I0564608

The Man of Middling Height

Middle East Literature in Translation

Michael Beard and Adnan Haydar, *Series Editors*

The Man of Middling Height

Fadi Zaghmout

Edited by
Fil Inocencio Jr.

Translated from the Arabic by
Wasan Abdelhaq

Afterword by
Cheryl Toman

Syracuse University Press

Content advisory: This book contains descriptions of sexual assault and violence. Please read with care.

First published in Arabic by Dar al-Ahliyyah, Amman, 2021, as *Ebra Wa Kushtuban*.

ISBN: 9780815611851 (paperback)

9780815657439 (e-book)

Library of Congress Cataloging-in-Publication Data

Names: Zaghmūt, Fādī author | Abdelhaq, Wasan translator | Inocencio, Fil, Jr. editor | Toman, Cheryl writer of afterword

Title: The man of middling height / Fadi Zaghmout ; edited by Fil Inocencio Jr. ; translated from the Arabic by Wasan Abdelhaq ; afterword by Cheryl Toman.

Other titles: Ibrah wa-kushtubān. English

Description: First edition. | Syracuse, New York : Syracuse University Press, 2025. | Series: Middle East literature in translation | Includes bibliographical references.

Identifiers: LCCN 2025008274 (print) | LCCN 2025008275 (ebook) | ISBN 9780815611851 paperback | ISBN 9780815657439 ebook

Subjects: LCGFT: Queer fiction | Romance fiction | Fiction | Novels

Classification: LCC PJ7976.A323 I2713 2025 (print) | LCC PJ7976.A323 (ebook) | DDC [Fic]—dc23

LC record available at https://lccn.loc.gov/2025008274

LC ebook record available at https://lccn.loc.gov/2025008275

The authorized representative in the EU for product safety and compliance is Mare Nostrum Group B.V. Mauritskade 21D, 1091 GC Amsterdam, The Netherlands

gpsr@mare-nostrum.co.uk

Contents

Author's Note

Our Arab societies suffer from a masculine dominance that has distorted the natural balance of human relationships. Men enjoy numerous privileges in various aspects of life at the expense of women, who have had their freedoms restricted and bodily rights stripped away. We have developed a societal construct in which all human traits are reduced, divided, and distributed according to one's biological binary sex; one mold for men, another for women.

I am not here to enumerate the horrors our societies endure as a result of this difficult cultural legacy. I do not intend to dedicate this book's introduction to the humiliating statistics about women's participation in public life in various Arab countries (Arab States Civil Society Organizations and Feminists Network 2021), the frightening numbers of women that speak of violence directed against them, their lack of inclusion and empowerment, and the discrimination they face in different aspects of life. Everyone should be aware of these facts.

However, I also believe that a collective consciousness is beginning to form, one that cares about women's rights and gender equality. But as a feminist activist interested in gender issues, I recognize the difficulty of explaining the changing ideas around gender to the general public. Both feminist theory and the reexamination of gender itself are unfamiliar and challenging to the prevailing cultural norms.

The general public does not distinguish between biological sex and gender as a social construct; between male and female as biological attributes, and man and woman as social attributes. The Arabic language, however, (similar to the English language) has words to distinguish between these two structures and has had them since its inception, thousands of years before the emergence of feminist theory. There is a word specifically for describing male as a biological descriptor (zakar, ذكر) and another word for describing man as a social type (rajol, رجل). Within the structure of Arabic, it is not permissible to substitute one for the other to give the same meaning.

From this linguistic distinction came the idea of the novel. Since gender division is created by a set of traits built upon a single biological attribute—that is, sex—why not try to imagine the development of this division in a different way? What if, instead of sex, we combined different traits and distributed them among people based on another biological attribute?

Height, for example?

What would this society look like?

Certainly, there are many factors that play a role in shaping gender. It has a biological aspect, but it has also evolved alongside human consciousness and through its interaction with the surrounding cultural environment. Further, it is crystalized within the linguistic vessel that hosts this consciousness. I tried to address these various aspects of gender's formation while creating a unique world. The Arabic language, however, created some specific challenges in this endeavor.

Arabic language is a "gendered" language, with its grammatical constructions having gender classifications. Its pronouns are masculine and feminine and its plurals as well, and its words are feminized with the presence of the feminine letter "ta" (ة) or the letter "noon" (ن) of the feminine plural at their ends, and masculinized in their absence. Even inanimate objects are given a gendered dimension in Arabic. We say "this is a chair" (هذا كرسي) (masculine) and "this is a table" (هذه طاولة) (feminine). This demonstrates the importance of language in shaping collective consciousness and the gender identity of individuals.

If I were to imagine a world where gender has developed differently, it would be necessary for this world to speak a different language. If I wanted to give this world its due right, I had to write this story using that language: a language that is engraved with height division.

However, creating an entirely new language is difficult, and even if done successfully, and a story is written in that language, who among the readers would understand it?

I found a solution that I believe served the progress of the story. I leave it in the hands of the readers to judge. I wrote the novel in Arabic in hope that it receives readers' approval and helps raise public awareness on gender issues. Translating it into English added another layer of complexity to the story. I worked closely with the editor to tailor the gender references to suit the English language, which is a language that is known to be less gendered than Arabic but still has gender engraved in its pronouns and vocabulary.

As the French feminist philosopher Simone de Beauvoir says in her famous book, *The Second Sex* (1949, 2011), "One is not born, but rather becomes, a woman." (Beauvoir, 330). In this imagined world, this might become, "One is not born tall, but rather becomes so." Similarly, inspired by the words of the American feminist philosopher Judith Butler in *Gender Trouble* (1990, 2006), who considers gender a performative act, I wanted the characters to express their "gender" or let's say "social type" through their interactions with their environment, to reveal themselves through their own personal conflicts with their surroundings and with the social divisions of their world.

I wish you an enjoyable reading experience.

Best regards,
Fadi Zaghmout

Works Cited

Arab States Civil Society Organizations and Feminists Network. 2021. "Women's Economic Justice and Rights in the Arab Region." July 2021. https://arabstates.unwomen .org/sites/default/files/Field%20Office%20Arab%20States

/Attachments/2021/07/Womens%20Economic%20Justice
%20and%20Rights-Policy%20Paper-EN.pdf.

Beauvoir, Simone. 1949, 2011. *The Second Sex*. Translated by
Constance Capisto-Borde. Vintage Books.

Butler, Judith. 1990, 2006. *Gender Trouble: Feminism and the
Subversion of Identity*. Routledge.

Acknowledgments

I would like to express my heartfelt gratitude to the University of Alabama for their generous subvention, which helped make the publication of *The Man of Middling Height* possible. My deepest thanks go to Professor Cheryl Toman, whose steadfast support and encouragement from the very beginning has meant more to me than words can express. Her belief in this project has been a source of inspiration, and I am honored to have her insightful afterword grace these pages.

I am immensely thankful to Wasan Abdelhaq, the gifted translator who brought my words to life in English with sensitivity and skill. Her work has been instrumental in making this book accessible to a broader audience. I am also grateful to my dear friend Fil Inocencio Jr. for his meticulous editorial assistance, lending his keen eye to help refine the manuscript before its submission to Syracuse University Press.

To the team at Syracuse University Press, my sincere thanks for your unwavering efforts in bringing this book to life in its best possible form. Your dedication to excellence has enriched this work, and I am deeply appreciative of the care and expertise you've invested in every detail.

Thank you all for being a part of this journey; your contributions have made this book richer, and I am honored to share this work with you by my side.

The Man of Middling Height

Prologue

Once I realized my need to pour out my love for Tallan on paper, I knew I didn't want to write it in our spoken language. I refuse to honor the unjust vocabulary, which denies his existence and fails to find a suitable pronoun to define him. I detest the structure and rules of that language which deliberately revolve around height; to celebrate shortness as the ultimate gift, or to denounce tallness as a haunting curse.

Ours is a divisive language revolving around shorts and talls, ruthlessly and irrevocably discarding all those who fall in between.

That is why, today, I will tell you my story in a new tongue, in a language that doesn't concern itself with height.

A language that embraces and celebrates gender.

This is a language designed to be more just to him and more deserving of the love story that unites the two of us. I am aware that, by using this language, I am creating for him a different world from the one he and I inhabit. I am also aware that, in doing so, I'm hurting others, treating them unjustly. But they don't concern me. All I want, in sharing my story, is to let it live and breathe in a different language—a language of an imaginary world.

A world in which my beloved is welcome.

1

As If I Were Reborn

The best love stories begin with a crack in the door.

I am referring to those mythical love stories that unfold without prior planning or knowledge at the moment when fate places the beloved in our path. When he stands behind that solid board, waiting silently, unaware that the door in front of him is nothing but a grand gateway transporting him from one life to another.

As if he were reborn.

On the other side of the door stood the other half of this love story. I paused for a moment, puzzled, as he pounded on the door.

"Who is it?"

No answer came.

I reached for the doorknob, not knowing that what awaited me would turn my life upside down. And, as cautious as I was in trying to avoid the bitterly cold weather outside, my hands had a different idea; they opened the door wide, so that I faced someone I had met only in my most intimate dreams.

As if I, too, started a new life.

It didn't occur to me that this was the moment I was reborn, and it didn't occur to him, either, that my being was pouring right into his heart. Our love story started without either of us realizing it. It started with a confusion that tinted it throughout.

Despite the intensity of the initial gaze my eyes bestowed upon him, I failed to perceive the enchantment concealed within his depths. My emotions toward him only solidified after a second and third glance, and perhaps a fourth, revealing to me that what I saw before me that day had the power to weaken my heart, shake my knees, and soften my soul.

I would have sent him away if it weren't for the sadness I spotted in his eyes. And so I surrendered, opened the door as wide as possible, and said, "Hi."

He replied in a gentle voice, "Good evening."

2

I Saw More of Him under the Light

Perhaps my response was too quick. "Good evening to you," I replied, my eyes twinkling in the moonlight.

With a bold confidence and a broad smile, he reached out his hand toward me. This unorthodox move caught me by surprise as talls are not allowed to shake hands with us short ones, but still, I shook his hand, hoping none of the neighbors would see me.

I politely asked him to enter through the door to the right, the one designated for talls. I then went back into the house, stepping into the room where we welcomed them. I was eager to discover the reason for his unplanned visit. It was past their curfew and typically talls weren't allowed to go out by themselves at such a time.

"Would you like to have some tea? Or perhaps you prefer coffee?"

As a tall, his preference was for tea. So tea it was.

He remained standing in the middle of the room, allowing me to see more of him. Under the light, I could see him more clearly, and I realized there was something odd about his features. Yes, he was tall, but he was more of a medium height, rather than significantly above average.

He definitely stood somewhere in the middle, between talls and shorts. He was neither thin like talls nor bulky like shorts. His head was shaved, following the customary practice of talls; a finely drawn line of golden henna started on his forehead and moved down to where his brows met, complementing his wide, warm hazel eyes—a clear sign of his refined background. He wore a traditional light-blue gown beneath a wool coat that didn't fully cover his broad stature.

I noticed he didn't take his shoes off at the door.

I hesitated for a moment, but then thought, "Well, if he is brazen enough not to take off his shoes, which is our custom, then I won't be shy about asking him to do it."

I have strong views on wearing shoes indoors. Taking off your shoes at the door keeps the house's energy and ambiance pure and clear. I knew that talls didn't like it, but I asked him to do so anyway, pointing to the door.

He politely apologized, then slowly and shamefully walked to the door and took them off.

In that moment, I stood astounded by what I saw. He was not even that tall!

And no! He was not a short, either.

He was clearly one of those who stood in the middle ground.

Inside, I was shivering. All through my forty years on this earth, I had never met a medium. As a dressmaker, I've spent the last twenty years designing gowns that accentuate the beauty of a bulky short and of a slender tall—never once doing so for a person of middle height.

I had only heard tales about these people, whose genes had gone haywire, shoving them in with the cursed and deformed—the ones we avoid so that we won't be afflicted by their evil spirits.

I wanted to kick him out and burn some sage to clear the air, but he noticed the fear in my eyes. He paused for a moment, pulled a bouquet of white jasmine from his jacket, and smiled in an attempt to calm me.

I took the flowers with a smile in return, asked him to sit down, and told myself to relax. We both sat in our designated spots, me on the wide sofa and him on the narrow chair. As he relaxed, he started to tell me his story.

3

Something about His Height Made Me Attracted to Him Like a Moth to the Light

"Please accept my apologies. I know it's a bit awkward to visit at this hour, but it was the only time I could sneak out by myself. I know you don't take clients at night, but I thought I might be lucky this time. I hope I'm not burdening you." He paused for a moment in an attempt to read my face. Then he introduced himself, "My name is Tallan."

He seemed to expect me to laugh, as the name contradicted reality. "Not so aptly named, I know."

I laughed and nodded, signaling him to go on with his story.

"As a teenager, I assumed I would be taller, since my height surpassed that of a short. But for some reason, my body was done. I realized I was clearly in this mid-range for good."

He took a breath. "Back then, we lost my father, and my mother went through a period of financial unrest. This made it hard for her, a depressed widow, to pay any attention to my height and to fix it with growth hormones."

He stopped one more time before he continued his story. "Our family, the Skys, helped us through this crisis, and we managed to regain our footing financially, but my height remained the one catastrophic happening that we couldn't fix or handle in any way. It was hard on my mother, since I was her favorite. She repeatedly refused to shun me or send me to live abroad, as everyone around her suggested."

He paused again, then reluctantly added, "My mother had been through something like this before with her brother, who was also of middling height, and that was before the government got firmer in coming to grips with height-related killings. The family sent him abroad in the way that wealthy families used to do, in order to escape the harsh reality and those sorts of crimes."

Finally he stopped talking, as if he felt he had revealed more than he should have.

I felt embarrassed on my part; numerous questions were swirling in my mind that I wanted to ask him, but I wasn't sure if it was appropriate or not. I wanted to know why his height stopped at that point. Did it affect his mental abilities or his psychological state? Was what happened to him a divine punishment for his parents, or maybe a personal punishment for him? Or was his average height a biological, hereditary condition in their family?

I was familiar with his family, a well-known family in the country—the wealthiest of the wealthy, with significant political influence. Some of them regularly visited me, appreciating my distinctive work and my name shining among designers specializing in royal attire. It was known about this family that its members lacked physical beauty. They were not distinguished by towering height, and none of them had an extremely short stature. However, this did not pose any difficulties for them because their wealth overshadowed any concerns about their physical appearance, and the public remained oblivious to the fact that their members were closer to average height.

Perhaps Tallan was indeed the least attractive among the members of that family according to public taste. Still, on that day, I did not see it. I felt that something about his average height was strangely appealing to me. I admired his frankness and openness, and I was charmed by the elegance of his speech and his overall sophistication. I loved his wide and clear eyes and felt him to be a child bewildered by the cruelty of the world. Therefore, I found myself apologizing to him and sincerely asking, "I'm sorry to hear your story. How can I help you?"

"My mother passed away a few months ago after a long battle with illness. She used to take care of my affairs and arrange private meetings for me with important service providers, such as those related to clothing design. After her death, my connection with the family tailor was severed, and I heard that he had left the country. I searched for another tailor and knocked on the doors of some of the top designers in the country."

I finished his sentence by saying, "and they refused to deal with you."

"Yes, even though I offered them large amounts in return."

I fell silent, pondering what he said after revealing the reason for his visit, as I wasn't prepared to confront such a situation. I don't usually like to delve into problems and sensitive matters. I believe in the saying, "Close the door that allows the wind to pass through, and have peace of mind."

He wasn't just of average height; that's something that could be concealed. He was also unmarried, as indicated by the vertical henna line drawn on his forehead. Being single myself and having a horizontal henna line on my forehead, I refused to receive unmarried talls alone in my house without a chaperone, to maintain my reputation as a seamstress and the respect of my customers and neighbors for me and my work.

I looked at him and asked, "And you're here because?" I didn't finish my sentence because I wanted him to answer for himself.

"Because I need a garment," he said. "I have an important wedding for one of my relatives, and I don't want to miss it. I need a garment that makes me appear taller, hides the width of my shoulders and the bulkiness of my limbs. I want to look natural at the wedding so that my relatives won't be embarrassed by me. I dream of appearing beautiful, capturing everyone's attention, and feeling the admiration and amazement of the attendees."

I felt sorry for him as he expressed his wishes to me. He had a beautiful face and captivating eyes like I had never seen before. However, I understood the average height of his stature, and I knew that what he was asking for, even if achieved superficially, wouldn't be real. It was as if he wanted to deceive himself before deceiving others, wanting to live someone else's life rather than his own.

It reminded me of the plight of the little chick in children's stories who couldn't accept the reality that its kind couldn't fly. It secretly wished to grow up to become an eagle soaring through the skies and playing with its clouds. One day, it convinced itself that it could fly, climbed to the top of the mountain, stood on its edge, spread its small wings, took a deep breath to fill its tiny lungs, and jumped from a great height, mimicking the eagle and believing with all its might that it could fly. However, fate betrayed it because its wings lacked the necessary strength to carry it in flight. It plummeted to the ground at lightning speed, crashing into the rocks, breaking its bones and ending its life in less than a second.

I paused for a moment, reconsidering the analogy in my mind, feeling that it wasn't a perfect match for what Tallan was going through. Although he seemed dreamy like that little chick, I realized I had unfairly compared him. Unlike the chick, he was actually rejected by his own kind. He was asked to possess abilities far from his nature as one of the essential components of defining his social type.

It's sad when someone wishes to have abilities beyond their nature, but it's even more miserable when they're required to possess those abilities as a fundamental aspect of what defines their social type and beauty. Although I knew then that all I could do was participate in his game to achieve some of his dreams, even if they were unreal and temporary, I felt something compelling me toward it, and a desire to help him took hold of me.

Just like him, I loved the idea of possessing magical abilities that beautify reality and deceive onlookers.

After a moment of contemplation, I replied, "I don't mind working with you, Tallan, but I cannot have you here alone, and I won't accept your presence in the late evening hours."

4

I Didn't Want to Confess That a New Moon Had Entered My Orbit

Rocky, my assistant, knew that I had feelings for Tallan even before I did. She knew me too well and could read all my expressions.

Although she was closed-minded, much like the rock she was named for, she was still witty, energetic, and fast-paced—despite her dense figure. She had big breasts and she was short, with thick thighs and chunky behind, yet she managed to move around so lightly that she looked like a hummingbird.

Right after Tallan left the talls' room, she snuck up behind me, covered my eyes with her palms, and jokingly asked, "Who am I?"

I removed her hands, turned, and smiled at her before I asked, "What time is it, Rocky?"

She always teased me whenever she caught me lost in thought; now she pretended I had been bemused all night. "What time is it? It's nine thirty! Morning, Madam!"

"Morning, lovely!" I answered, playing along. "You're late," I teased her back.

She laughed. "Oh no, I was waiting for you to land! Where have you been, birdie?" Although I am more of a T-rex than a birdie.

I didn't answer. I was too shy to confess that a new moon had entered my orbit. I was about to fly off into a world where I dreamed of Tallan.

"I know that look," she said, ambushing me, not giving me time to consider my answer.

I kept evading until she bluntly asked if I liked him. Then I gave up. "I'm still not sure," I said, even though I knew she wouldn't believe me.

"But relationships with clients are a red line. You've been through this before with your ex."

I promised her that I had learned my lesson well, but nothing could make her believe me.

"Anyhow, I don't know what you see in him."

I didn't want to confess to her or anyone that what attracted me mostly was actually his average height. I was in denial, and I could only imagine how she might react if I gave such an answer. I could see her getting furious, her eyes almost popping off her face and her mouth twisting up like a pretzel. I could imagine her fury, her disgust, and her awe at what I'd say. Not only that, I was sure she would start calling me a devil's minion. I didn't need all that drama. But I was baffled by his existence and amazed at his story. And Rocky was not only my assistant, but also my best friend and my closest confidant.

Although she was late for dinner with her spouses, I wanted to tell her Tallan's tale.

"Did you notice anything strange about our guest?"

"Something other than his surprise visit, by himself, at an inappropriate time for talls, and the fact that you allowed him to enter?" she asked sarcastically. "If any of my family had done that, it would have been a disaster."

I didn't want to argue so I brought the conversation back to what I'd wanted to discuss before: "What about his height?"

She answered with disgust, "Mmmm, I noticed he was neither that tall nor that thin," adding, "a bit ugly."

"He is not!" I found myself defending him, while also knowing that what I was about to say would make him even uglier in her eyes. "Beauty is relative," I reminded her. And before she could interrupt me, I said, "Actually, he's shorter than he looks."

"Shorter than he looks? What do you mean?" Her pupils dilated. "Any shorter than he looks makes him a medium. Is he medium?"

I hesitated over my answer, because I was afraid of her reaction, but in any case she didn't wait for my answer. She took my silence as confirmation. "Oh Sun, have mercy!" Her eyes were about to explode right there in their sockets, as if some great misfortune had befallen her. She cried out, "What's wrong with you today? Have you gone mad, welcoming one of those people into your home? And you like him, too?"

I was used to her overreactions. "Calm down," I tried to keep my voice light. "Take a deep breath and calm down."

I knew that my calmness might provoke her, but also that she wouldn't go too far with me, since I was her boss.

But she was stubborn. She left the room, walking to the kitchen and returning after a few minutes with an incense burner in one hand, walking around while muttering phrases that would presumably repel demons.

I let her finish what she was doing, knowing in my heart she was a hopeless case. There was no point in telling her that I liked him. She wouldn't understand me. She wouldn't sympathize or accept him. Despite that realization, I found myself telling her his story after she had finished her fifth circuit around the room and climbed into the stubby seat that barely held her. She sat in front of me, breathing heavily as she listened to me.

I recounted the entire story, with all the details Tallan had told me. Despite my deep sympathy for him, he still confused me.

I expected her to be intrigued and ask questions, but she only heard what she wanted to hear. She wasn't ready to consider anything that was different from her personal convictions. She waited for me to finish my story and then said, "It's all nonsense. I don't believe a word of his story. Even if there's any truth in it, I still don't trust people like him, and I won't sympathize with him."

She leaped out of her seat as she looked at her watch, ignoring my look of disapproval. "I have to leave now. It's late." She raised her index finger in the air, nervously pointing at me. "And I promise you that you won't help this Tallan. You won't welcome him into this house after today."

5

He Came to Visit Hiding
in a Thick Green Dress

Tallan looked more like a short when he came to visit two days after his first visit, in secrecy, at midnight despite my warnings, and hiding within a thick green dress. I was expecting him to come in the morning as I asked him to, and I didn't know how to act. Rocky would have been in the house, and I was worried that if she learned about his visit, she would overreact, the neighbors would gather around, and a scandal would erupt at my doorstep.

But when I heard the knocking on the door, I knew it was him. I rushed to the door and looked through the peephole; it was indeed him.

He looked different to me today, unlike himself; completely different from the person who visited me a few days ago. He wasn't wearing a long blue dress. He didn't look slender. He was not wearing high-heeled shoes to look taller. This time he looked fuller, hidden under another thick garment he carried around his waist, tucking some pillows inside the dress to look fuller.

Despite all that, I recognized him immediately and did not hesitate to invite him in. His back was bent as though he intended to appear shorter, leaving a visible hump on his upper back. I later learned that the hump was a pillow buckled at both ends to the top of his back.

I opened the main door for him this time and smiled.

"I am sorry I am visiting at this time looking like this." He relaxed his back after we went to the guest room.

I rushed to help him pull the pillows off his dress so he could rest. He had four of them distributed on his sides, stomach, and upper back. And two others were hidden around his thighs and his lower back.

As we put the pillows aside, I assured him that I understood why he did this, although I was still confused about it and wary of the whole thing. I told him there was nothing to worry about. I thought he had probably walked to my place. It would be safer for him to leave his house disguised as a short at this time of the day than to do so as a tall. He must have walked from the outskirts of the city across the river, where lodges were made for tall, single adults like him. He had to go through the market district, the gardens, the narrow streets across family neighborhoods, and the staircases of the old city center to get here.

If he had left his house in the state in which he visited me the first time, he would have had to follow the blue track that closes on weekdays after eight in the evening. He would have been interrogated by the night shortpolice or would have fallen victim to harassment, beatings, and perhaps rape by gangs of shorts deployed across the dark gardens.

He took off his shoes at the door without shame or hesitation, now that he had revealed his actual height. His shoes weren't high-heeled this time. He was wearing ordinary, wide shoes, the type shorts wear.

I almost laughed when I saw him unfolding a long handkerchief that he had wrapped around his feet to thicken them to make it easier to walk in those shoes without having to adjust them with every step.

For me and my fellow shorts, feet are an extension of our bodies: chunky, well-rounded, and very thick. Tallan's feet were as slender as the feet of any tall; graceful and elegant.

As soon as he sat down on one of the shorts' sofas, he began to speak. "I gave you two days to think about the situation so that you don't feel pressured, and I am so happy that you understand. But before I begin, I would like to thank you for welcoming me again, despite my look today, disguising myself as a clown unworthy of trust or respect, even though I came to you without an appointment.

"I would like to express my gratitude for your generosity with . . ." He put his hand in the pocket of his dress. And as he did last time, he took out another jasmine bouquet and handed it to me.

I took it from him and smiled, staring into his eyes. "Thank you. Very tasteful."

"I love the smell of jasmine in the morning because it reminds me of my mother," he commented, smiling.

He added in a nostalgic tone of voice, "She would wake up at dawn with the rising sun and make us breakfast in the garden before we went to school."

Just like my dad did, I thought to myself. He brought back beautiful memories from my childhood when my father used to prepare breakfast for us before we went to school. My father was like his mother, a tall. They had to take on the chores of getting everyone up in the morning and making breakfast for the family.

It is known that talls are more sensitive to sunlight, so it was easier for them to do these morning errands, unlike shorts, who are most active at night. We, shorts, are proud to be children of the night since prehistoric times when our strong physique qualified us for the duties of protection in the dark. In the dark, sight was no longer important, so talls would rest until the break of dawn. In the sunlight, they woke up to arrange hunting gear and clean dishes shorts used during their sleeping hours. This was a natural and instinctive arrangement between the two social types, allowing them to complement each other. During that age, as evidenced by the excavations, the physical structure of us began to differentiate. Since talls consumed more resources than shorts, when food became scarce, damage to the social balance of primitive societies became inevitable. It left shorts weak and without adequate food, exposing the entire community to the danger of starvation, conflict among its members, and extinction. Therefore, with time, social dynamics shifted, and talls were urged to consume less food while shorts were encouraged to eat much more, which allowed them to become more dominant and powerful. After long centuries, and despite the change and development of societies and the availability of food, a tall's thin body and light weight remained two important signs that indicated their type and social role. And to this day, talls are still energetic in the morning, and shorts are more active at night.

"I also love the smell of jasmine." I grabbed the bouquet and put it in a vase. I carried it and headed to the kitchen and filled the vase with water. I quickly came back. "Tallan, I have a question." I paused pensively for a second, "Since you are not tall, nor are you short, what do you like? Night or day?"

The question surprised him. He laughed and looked thoughtful as he answered, as if no one had asked him this question before.

"Hmm . . . I honestly don't know." He paused. "I think I identify as a short in this aspect. I prefer night. Partly because I feel more energetic during the night hours. But I admit that I feel sad because my movement is restricted at night. I spend most nights at home or in the garden alone."

I was disheartened by what he said about restricting his movement. I hugged him, wanting to ease his sadness.

He accepted my embrace, then looked at me with gentle warmth after I withdrew.

"I am a typical shorty in this matter. I can't stand getting up early at all. And when I have to, I feel like someone hit my head with a stick, so I spend the rest of my day in a bad mood." I laughed and continued, "I love the night. Still, I spend most nights at home alone too. I am not social, and I don't have a lot of friends. I also like to work quietly when everyone goes to sleep and spend time with my fabrics, my scissors, my threads, and my thoughts."

I was silent for a moment before I added cheerfully, "But now you are my night partner for the coming period until we finish our project."

I rose and signaled for him to join me. "I want to show you some fabrics."

He followed me to the dressing room.

"I thought of some options that may suit you, but I prefer to take your body measurements before I show you." I hesitated a little and continued, "We can do it next time if you're not ready for that today."

I could sense his embarrassment, as he had to take off his clothes and stay in his underwear in order for me to take his measurements. Normally I would offer my clients leggings to wear instead of their usual robes while I took their sizes, so they wouldn't feel shy, but I didn't know if I had any suitable for him. I guessed that the talls' long, form-fitting pants would not fit his thighs, and the shorts' version would be too wide.

"No, no, I'm ready," he said excitedly. "We don't have enough time before the wedding. We may need to make a few alterations. I know my size is not standard, and I know that most tailors find it difficult to design something to fit me, so we need to start early."

He turned around, waiting for me to take out my fitting pants for him to put on.

I didn't want to make him feel uncomfortable. I paused for a moment, thinking about the right size for him. I headed toward the pants drawer and hastened to pull out the top one, which contained the shortest shorts' pants, believing that they also held the narrowest among them. I corrected myself and closed it again, then pulled out the drawer closest to the ground. I had to consider both length and width, assigning each drawer for a specific length range and dividing the space inside each drawer by the width of the pants.

Bending down, I retrieved the longest and widest pants. As I struggled to straighten my back, the motion didn't sit well with my spine. I realized once again that I had made a mistake; these pants would be too loose, and I wouldn't be able to take accurate measurements. Therefore, I had to endure the pain and bend again, pulling the longest and narrowest trousers located on the other side of the drawer. I had not used that size before because it was rare for me to find a short with such a size.

I then asked him to come into the changing room so that he could take off his clothes and put on the pants I gave him.

When he came back, I was relieved to see that they weren't too tight. But the sight of his bare chest aroused me instantly. It was as if the confused shape of his body, somewhere between talls and shorts, attracted me in a way I had not experienced before. I felt my head spinning, and I almost closed my eyes to protect myself from what I saw in front of me. I had to deal with my reaction so as not to embarrass myself in front of him. I apologized and ran to the kitchen to catch my breath. I drank a glass of cold water and opened the window to breathe.

I poured him a glass of orange juice and put some do-
nuts on a plate to justify my escape. I took a deep breath,
urging myself to breathe normally.

When I entered the room, he was standing with his
back to me, quietly examining the fabrics, allowing me
a few seconds to examine his torso. It was neither fat nor
slim, and I couldn't stop staring.

"Ready?" I smiled.

He shook his head and smiled in return. He seemed
more comfortable in his body than I could have imagined,
and I think that this confidence made me more attracted
to him. I picked up the measuring tape and approached
him. I asked him to stand up straight, and I measured
the distance between his shoulders and recorded it in my
notebook. Then I went down two fingers to measure the
width of his chest.

I admit that I found it strangely attractive. It was flat,
closer in look to talls' chests. Yet his flesh drooped slightly,
with two small nipples that looked as sweet as raisins, and
a scattering of soft hair. His proportions reminded me of
my last partner, but Tallan's chest was thicker and less
rounded than hers. I liked his more.

I ignored my feelings and proceeded with the measurements. I asked him to turn around so that I could
take the dimensions of his back. I signaled to him to lean
toward the right so that I could assess his waist, and was
impressed by a large mole that adorned the layer of fat on
his side. I asked him to stand up straight to note down the
width and circumference of his waist and laughed as I saw

him draw a breath, trying to flatten his little belly. I told him to relax before taking the final numbers.

Having finished with his upper body, I hesitated before continuing, fearing that my desire for him would take over as soon as I bent down to continue. I paused and drank some water.

Returning, I put the tip of the measuring tape on his waist and asked him to hold it. I leaned aside to pick up the other end and recorded the length of his legs. I asked him to part his legs so that I might measure the circumference of his thigh, which was somewhat large like the thighs of shorts, though longer and firmer like those of a tall. Perhaps he walked a lot or rode a bicycle daily. I realized that his thighs would be the most challenging part for me in designing the appropriate dress for him because it would be difficult to hide them in a tight, fitted dress. That didn't bother me because I was nervous trying to control my desire for him, especially with my hands roaming around his sensitive area. I didn't know whether he was self-conscious about me touching him or not. Was he trying to stop himself from having an erection?

I realized then that his body was betraying him, and I was confused as how to act. I was afraid that he would think I was molesting him or using my power and his need for my help to take advantage of him physically.

I hesitated, standing near him, trying to read his facial expressions so as not to do something that might alienate him.

But he surprised me with a kiss.

I could feel my heart beating fast as his lips met mine.

The force of those feelings that gripped me made me open my eyes for a moment. I spotted a shadow of someone standing behind the window and startled violently. I quickly sprang to the window, trying to see who the shadow was, but it had disappeared. I opened the window very violently and turned left and right, cursing nervously, without regard for the romantic moment that Tallan and I had just shared.

6

He Was the Hero in My Dream

I was ashamed of what had happened! I couldn't believe I had been that nervous! I didn't know how I allowed myself to shout out loud in front of Tallan when I caught the shadow of the person standing behind the window. Still, I left Tallan and chased after the intruder, unleashing my tongue to utter words unworthy of being repeated in front of a tall. After that proved fruitless, I returned to the house and got my pistol from my room. I went back to the window and fired several shots in the air to frighten the intruder, ignoring the presence of Tallan in my house.

He stood there silently, smiling despite his nervousness and in spite of the situation, as if he were politely telling me that my behavior was reckless and that the situation did not require such a violent reaction.

Although I was amazed at his calmness—because the danger to his life was greater than any danger that could have affected me—I did not comment. I went back to the window, closed it, and pulled the curtains. I apologized to him because I hadn't realized the curtains weren't drawn as usual, as Rocky always made sure they were secure before she left every evening. Could it be that she did it on purpose?

I banished that idea right away because it seemed so out of character. I also noted that the intruder was seemingly slender as they ran off fast at this hour. That made me more confused. Who was this tall who dared to go out at that hour of the night and approach my window to spy on us like that?

I asked Tallan if any of his companions were with him, but he affirmed he came by himself. Could it be my ex? I wondered. I knew she was shrewd and cunning, and that she still held a grudge long after I decided to end my relationship with her. But it was unlikely to be her. Although she had stalked me for a long time after our separation, she had since disappeared. I had also heard that she'd gotten engaged and that her wedding date was approaching.

I didn't know. I didn't want to think about it. There was an even greater desire within me that day. The kiss I shared with Tallan was more important than this trivial incident. It released strong feelings inside me. I held onto the sweetness of that moment. It had left me astonished.

I swear that I couldn't breathe when my lips touched his. I felt my body shivering. It was like a dream in which he was my hero. And my joy was greater because I was certain that he was living the same dream.

He approached me to shake hands after he had put his clothes back on. I held his hand for as long as possible and felt his grip tighten around mine. He hugged me as if there was something that would push us to hug a second, third, and fourth time. He kissed me passionately. Then he left.

He promised to return in two days at the same time.

"And to the same feelings," I whispered to myself.

7

We Are Not as Different
as You Like to Believe

I tend to believe that the world has a secret plan plotted in advance for everyone to expand their awareness of their surroundings smoothly and elegantly.

A few days after my meeting with Tallan, a new employee arrived. There was something unusual about him that I didn't fully understand until later. His name was Miles. It suited him well, as he was as tall as a palm tree. One of Rocky's spouses recommended that I hire him.

I had met him two days ago for a short while and loved his presence. I found him cheerful and light-hearted, just like Rocky. He seemed carefree, with zero responsibilities or concerns. His ideas and beliefs, like others of his age, were not solid. They formed and changed with the direction of the wind, making Miles seem pure and naive. But he was as talkative as if he had swallowed a radio as a child. Although I knew that his chattiness might annoy Rocky, it would not bother me because I love to gossip and hear people's stories, even if they are trivial and meaningless.

31

Both arrived as I was thinking of Tallan. I didn't notice them until Rocky started calling my name more than once and waving to me with both hands. I suddenly woke up when I noticed the palm of her hand that was about to hit my nose.

I coughed while laughing and welcomed them, "Welcome, Rocky and Miles." Miles with his straight stature. And Rocky as chunky as ever.

"Good morning."

"Good morning?!" Rocky said in a sarcastic tone. "You mean good evening!"

She reached out and pinched my chubby cheek and asked me as if I were her spoiled child, "Where are you, birdie?"

Miles laughed, as he did not expect to hear anyone of my size being called birdie.

I thought she chose this name for me because my hooked nose looked like a bird's beak. But she could also have meant lovebirds, thus mocking my attraction to Tallan.

Miles watched as Rocky moved her hands around my face and blabbered words that would presumably expel any evil spirits that roamed around me.

"Daydreaming is new to her," she said, directing her comment to Miles. "No?" She gave me a quick look, and I understood what she meant.

But Miles did not understand. He took the opportunity to start gossiping, "I have a friend like you. He is always daydreaming. He doesn't notice my words until I call him several times."

He kept talking without taking a breath or letting either of us comment on what he said. "Imagine that sometimes this happens while we are in the middle of a conversation! One time we were discussing the change of the official state flag. He asked me a question and then suddenly I lost him. It was as if he had moved to another world."

Miles moved his hands in a motion that indicated the cut-off of reception. "I didn't notice his absence because I didn't expect him to enter that state while I was talking to him, and I was responding to him with a lengthy reply. I was talking and talking, and after a while, he responded with an irrelevant answer. He was daydreaming. I had to grab his shoulders. I shook him so hard that he looked at me and asked me stupidly, what did you say?!"

Miles acted out his words instantly, moving around incessantly as if the friend he was talking about was in the room with us. He laughed as he was finishing his story, "I replied, nothing. I was asking you about the weather today."

I decided to change the topic to avoid Miles's long-winded comparison between me and his dreamy friend and asked him about his position on the change of the state's flag.

I knew the flag was a sensitive topic for Rocky. She was angry with the results of the public vote that took place last week. She didn't like the government's acceptance of the revolutionary change that the *League of Talls' Advocates* had proposed by adding blue vertical stripes to it.

The subject appears to have been important to Miles as well. He picked up my question at lightning speed and started talking passionately as if it meant life or death for him, "I was advocating for this change."

Rocky got angry and wanted to comment, but Miles didn't give her a chance. "With all due respect to everyone's national affiliation and to all opinions that adhere to traditions. With my understanding of the modern history of the flag and the nation's connection to it as a symbol that unites us all, I felt that the symbol was incomplete and unfair to an important group that represents half of society. This is something everyone who voted for change can agree on."

He moved before us as if he were a defense attorney in court and asked, "How do we ignore the fact that the flag was covered in green circles and had not a single blue stripe?"

I knew Rocky was eager to reply. She attacked him sharply, "You young people do not know the significance of the symbol, and you do not know your history. You do not appreciate our traditions. You are easily dragged behind foreign fads without regard to your reality."

She continued accusing him as if she were a public prosecutor, "Tell us, Professor Miles. How did changing the flag help us?"

"First of all, it's not a foreign fad. Talls represent half of society. We did so in the past and will continue to do so in the future. We have the right to demand equality and justice and to be represented in all national symbols," he answered her confidently and steadfastly.

"What equality and justice are you talking about?" Rocky shook her head in disapproval. "Is it fair to equate things that are completely different?" And before he could answer, she added, "We all know that our society is the fairest of all places in our treatment of talls. Enough of these destructive thoughts!"

"But we are not as different as you imagine." He surprised us with his objection, then explained to us what he meant, "I'll give you an example. We all have the same stomach and the same digestive system. Right?"

We both were silent, Rocky and I. We nodded in agreement, trying to understand what he was getting at.

"Why then do many families still serve two plates to shorts at every meal and only one plate to talls?" he asked innocently.

We laughed at his example, which we did not expect. I commented, "It looks like you are hungry and haven't had any breakfast yet." But Rocky couldn't let it pass, so she corrected the information, saying, "You are right, we have the same stomach. But modern science proved that the stomach of shorts is larger than the stomach of talls. So it is obvious that shorts need more food than talls."

"But," Miles said, "recent studies indicate that the human stomach is like rubber, and it expands with the amount of food consumed."

I had actually read this study and was convinced of it. But I suspected that Rocky hadn't read it yet and even if she had, it wouldn't have changed her mind. She likely heard of it and considered it some kind of scientific misinformation that sought to destabilize our society and distort the natural balance between shorts and talls.

Rocky became impatient and raised her voice at Miles, "Are you suggesting that we give both talls and shorts the same amount of food?"

"Why not?"

"Do you want us to distort the natural order of things so that talls become fat and shorts turn lean? Do you realize how destructive that would be to our society? To the existing social system?"

"I am not advocating for that," said Miles, defending himself, "but I demand the freedom of the individual to choose the amount of food they need and desire, irrespective of their body type. Their height shouldn't be an issue."

"Shouldn't be an issue?" Rocky's voice was full of anger. "Are you crazy? It seems you forgot the greedy talls and the famines and diseases that plagued our primitive societies. We wouldn't be where we are today without awareness of our different bodies, without realizing the different needs of our body types. Divine wisdom requires observing the nature of both types and preserving what distinguishes each of them. Can you imagine tall weak bodies capable of carrying all that extra weight?"

"You are right! How can I forget the greedy talls?" Miles's response surprised both of us. "Those stories terrified me when I was a kid. My mom used to scare me by saying she would leave me with our greedy tall neighbor if I didn't do my homework. He looked weird with all that extra weight. They told me later, when I grew up, that he had a thyroid problem, but we were convinced it was evil spirits."

He was silent for a moment, then asked a question. "What if we served the same number of plates for both talls and shorts, but with more food on the shorts' plates? This is how we can be just to both without risking the spread of gluttony among talls."

That was what many modern families already do, but traditional families refused to abandon their customs. In fact, changing the habit wouldn't have made a difference because superficial equality affects the external form of the process, not its essence. Rocky, a conservative by nature, insisted on being served two plates at every meal even if she wasn't hungry. Yet, her tall spouses only got one plate each. And if, for some reason, they didn't eat all of it, Rocky would finish off what remained.

"Every family is free to choose the way the plates are distributed among its members, but I choose to stick to our traditions in order not to confuse the younger generations," she said, trying to sound tolerant of opposing views. She paused for a moment, then asked Miles, "Have you ever compared a tall who is pregnant with a short?"

The difference was obvious, of course, but Miles asked her, "What is the difference?"

"The tall spends nine months pregnant while sick and unable to move. Sometimes she gives birth before her due date. And a large percentage of talls actually lose their pregnancies.

"As for shorts," she continued, "the shape of their bodies allows them to endure pregnancies as they hardly change."

That wasn't true at all. Many shorts have exhausting pregnancies, and some lose their babies before birth. But that is never mentioned because shorts should always be portrayed as tough and strong. Her words provoked me, and I couldn't stop myself from interfering. I was fully aware of the hyperbole of Rocky's claim. I know the reality because my mom, despite her short body, had very difficult pregnancies. Meanwhile, my tall aunt was giving birth to one child after the other, smoothly and easily.

My mother gave birth to me in the seventh month of her pregnancy, and I was small in size. Weakness accompanied me in the first years of my life and Mother's attempts to make me chubby, like the other children my age, all seemed to fail. I remembered how my tall grandmother used to pray for me to grow up to be a tall because she had lost all hope that my body would store any fat. She would have preferred me to be short and fat, of course. But if that weren't possible, then being tall and thin was much better than being a scrawny short. Or even worse, River forbid, a medium-sized person.

The family was worried in my early teens when my body seemed out of proportion. That's when my dad started focusing on roasting potatoes. He forced me to eat them at all meals until my body started to swell and grow thicker.

"It is not true what you are saying," I scolded Rocky. "Despite the weakness of talls compared to shorts, their ability to endure pregnancies is not different from shorts. This was proven by all recent studies. The idea that both talls' and shorts' pregnancies are safe was what the government and human rights groups were trying to spread across conservative societies where talls' pregnancies were not welcomed."

Rocky wanted to answer, but I interrupted her, "Let's end this pointless discussion. We have a lot to do today."

I asked her to teach Miles how to prepare breakfast and asked Miles to shadow Rocky all week long so he could learn the craft. Rocky looked like she wanted to continue the argument, but eventually her anger subsided and she did what I asked. I also asked her to show me some blue fabrics in order to start designing Tallan's gown.

Then I went into my room to daydream about him.

8

As If Our Souls Have Known
Each Other Forever

My relationship with Tallan developed rapidly after our first kiss. He visited me every evening and accompanied me through the hours of the night, until dawn, when he left. He came to me every time in the form of a short, with a bouquet of white jasmine hidden in his jacket. He would present it to me after taking off his shoes at the entrance to the house, and look into my eyes with a smile. I would take up the bouquet and hurry to put it in a vase alongside the flowers from the previous night. I found the romantic gesture irresistible, gratified by the persistence it revealed. I waited for him every night. Counted the flowers again the next day.

As the barriers between us dissolved, I began to meet that bouquet of flowers with a hug and two kisses, one on the cheek and the other on the lips.

That first kiss had changed everything between us. We had shifted from customer and shopkeeper to secret partners. And although neither of us understood what was happening, we both felt it. It felt as if we had known

each other for a long time. As if our souls had been connected for ages. Eventually, we became eager to dive into
those feelings that our first kiss had revealed.

That night, our meeting began just like all of our
other meetings. I asked about his day and he asked about
mine. We discussed the progress of the dress I was making, choosing details and refining the proportions. Previously, we had maintained our self-control, but on that
fateful night, the closeness of our bodies and the intimacy
we had built over our nights together took over. Our un-
spoken desire for each other became overwhelming. It
only took us minutes to find ourselves wrapped in each
other's arms. I loved the sensation of my short, thick arms
around his waist, clinging to his slender, bent frame while
he embraced me with long, graceful arms. I reached up to
feel his shaved head, pulling him close. He leaned down,
kissing my neck with a passion that thrilled me.

I loved the feeling of his naked body. I was aroused by
the differences in our bodies and the contrasting forms
of our genitals. I led him to the bed by his wrist, then laid
my sturdy body over him, and wrapped my brown, fleshy
legs around his muscular, sinewy thighs. I grabbed his
head firmly to kiss him, and my long, curly hair spread
out like a fleeting shadow to cover the spectacle of our
bodies joined together in desire.

Although the differences between our bodies were
new to me, Tallan satisfied me in a way that was both
unfamiliar and irresistible. I wondered if it was because
of his compromised social status or, perhaps, his physical
abnormalities?

Something in his weakness made me more attracted to him. As if by being with me, he was giving himself to me. As if I was now responsible for him; to protecting and defending him. I could also feel something powerful about him that moved me. I didn't know its source. Perhaps it was the firm tone of his voice, his confident manner of speaking, or his elegance and sophistication. Either way, he captivated my heart.

These unexpected contradictions added excitement to our relationship. His presence made me feel strong and weak at the same time and I think I evoked the same feelings in him. The most beautiful moments were those that followed our sexual union, when I held his hand and stared into his wide, fathomless eyes. I was overwhelmed by gratitude that such happiness could exist.

Even still, I wondered if I would let him down. What if I couldn't find the strength to stand up to the world and confess my love for him? To shout out loud, proclaiming in front of everyone, "I love you, Tallan."

9

Neither a Needle nor a Thimble

Patience is one of the things I learned as a dressmaker, in addition to appreciating life's small pleasures that we get as a result of simple, easy victories; the ones where your heart fills with peace, your eyes widen, and you find yourself smiling involuntarily.

One of my proudest victories is that I am able to seamlessly insert the narrow silk thread through the needle, and pull it through the other side without fear of it slipping back. I perform these actions tens of times a day; so often it has become automatic. Yet it never loses its magic for me, even on the busiest days when I am rushed, I still find a space to indulge in this magical feeling of victory.

In those rare moments when I am left to work in silence, that simple act gives me joy. I hold the needle between the stocky forefinger and thumb of my right hand, the thread trailing behind it. My other hand holds a part of a garment that drapes comfortably across my lap. My right index finger secures the needle; my left is covered by a thimble. Almost unconsciously, these two humble pieces of metal work together to create something powerful and meaningful. With the help of a length of fine thread, they

43

are able to take a formless piece of cloth and shape it in any way I desire. Using just a needle and a thimble, I can create a garment that adds to and shapes the identity of its wearer in any number of ways.

I thought, then, of my time with Tallan. The second time he visited me. I was working with the needle in one hand and the thimble in the other. His presence planted a seed within me; ideas I had never considered before. His strange and shameful height provoked thoughts in my mind that bothered me—ideas about our identities, roles, divisions, and social classifications. These elements determined so much of our lives; the clothes we were supposed to wear, the shape of our bodies, our attitudes, habits, and traditions.

I had a moment of inspiration as I held the fine needle in my right hand. I moved it aside and caressed the surface of the thick thimble on the index finger of my left hand, thinking of how each of those items mirrored the workings of our everyday lives.

I paused, trying to bring order to the thoughts wandering through my mind.

What I learned in my younger years was that both the needle and the thimble are necessary; they complete each other's work. One cannot succeed without the other and together they can create almost anything. In this, I felt it was exactly like our social fabric. It cannot exist or function without the cooperation of both talls and shorts.

My thoughts shifted and I found myself thinking about Tallan and how he was neither tall nor short.

He was not like a needle.

Nor was he a thimble.

Thus, he was not fit to play a role in the construction of our social fabric. I suddenly remembered what I had learned as a child about the beginning of creation and what the scriptures taught about talls and shorts; how they must intermarry, and how their distinctive statures complemented each other and allowed them, together, to construct the earth. And yet there I was, drawn to Tallan, a creature that violated all those beliefs. He represented an anomaly; neither short nor tall. What role could he play in our society? Why does he exist?

I remembered then, what he had said about his absence from hormonal treatment sessions in his adolescence. It took me back to those days in my childhood when I first started to realize the relationship between talls and shorts.

Up until a certain age, we are all alike: We study together. We play together. Our clothes are dyed the same yellow color. We carry innocent names. Our categorization process usually begins in our early teenage years, although a few of us grow faster and easily reach the three cubits and six palms threshold. Whoever reaches that height is taken to the psychologist. There, they are taught about the social role expected of them and the rapid physical changes that will affect their bodies while undergoing growth hormone sessions.

My best friend at primary school, Clara, was the first to reach three cubits and six palms. I remember we knew she was the tallest among us, but we didn't yet understand what that meant or how it would shape us socially.

That day, the school principal—a short—entered our classroom, accompanied by the tall psychologist. He called Clara's name out loud and asked her to gather her things. He picked up her bag before accompanying her to his office. All day I waited for her to come back and finish the painting that we were making together. But that never happened. She didn't come back that day, and she didn't come back the next day, or ever again. I spent many months alone, unable to find new friends to compensate for her absence. I tried calling her one evening, but I was not allowed to speak to her. Instead, I listened, surprised, to her father ordering me not to call her until I had reached the limit of height with which I would be identified for the rest of my life. I cried and begged him to at least let me hear her voice. Something I said must have touched him, because he let me have one last conversation with her.

I asked her what happened the day she disappeared.

She told me how the psychiatrist took her to his room to prepare her for the next stage of her life. He gave her a metallic bag containing a blue dress and a cylindrical box of ceremonial henna with which to draw the initial vertical line on her forehead. In addition, he gave her some pamphlets that carried general instructions to help guide her in the coming days. He then asked her to take off the yellow dress that all children wore and change into the new, blue one. Afterward, he gave her a strong hug.

"Congratulations," he said. "You have become tall."

He then told her that she would no longer go to her school but would go on a year-long break to continue her growth process. If necessary, she might also undergo hormonal therapy to encourage greater height. Once she had reached the prescribed four cubits, she would go to a different school; one designated specifically for talls.

She was also asked to consult with her family in order to choose a new name that suited her newly confirmed social type. They chose the name Cloudia, associating her with the height and beauty of being adrift in the sky.

The psychologist laid out a set of rules and social norms to which she was required to adhere from that moment forward. He summarized it by repeating the three most important rules of being a tall:

First: Unless they are family, you should avoid
     socializing with shorts in public places as per
     tradition.
Second: It is necessary to monitor your diet in order
     to maintain the body composition and physical
     proportions that are appropriate for your height.
     Being tall and obese is socially frowned upon.
Third: You must train yourself to speak in a soft
     tone of voice. Loud voices are not for talls.

As for myself and the rest of the students who had not yet reached three cubits and six palms, nothing much changed except that we lost our old friends and made new ones from neighboring classes who were fortunate to stay short like us. We continued our studies as usual until we graduated from high school, where it was finally acknowledged that our growth had stopped and that we were below the cut-off limit.

The last months at school held the most beautiful memories for me, especially when we understood that we were destined to be shorts, and we began to look forward to our new social role and to the social advantages that we were about to be given. We were overwhelmed with pride when they replaced our yellow dresses with the green ones associated with the earth, just as the blue garments worn by talls related to the sky.

Celebrations were held for many nights and days, marked by lavish feasts to help us gain more weight and become closer to the ideals of shortness.

10

Oh, Sun! Have Mercy

I stood in front of the shelf of blue fabrics, trying to pick the right shade for the dress I was designing for Tallan. I usually lean toward using trendy dark blue colors for talls' dresses. Occasionally I turn to the ambiguous turquoise shades that work for dresses of both talls and shorts for special occasions, such as elegant weddings, fashion shows, and liberal social circles. However, I hesitated about using the turquoise color for Tallan's dress because I wanted him to look taller than he was. I needed to accentuate his height and elegance.

I decided not to take any risk with the color. I made up my mind and picked a fabric of a deep and pure blue; the color of a clear day. I chose the highest quality silk to match the social status of Tallan's family and to ensure that he stood out among the attendees.

I placed it on the design table and headed toward the shelf of warm-colored fabrics. I wanted to add some of those colors to the dress to give it a touch of glamour and luxury. Incorporating such colors into the final design of long dresses was no longer unconventional in weddings.

These events broke the norms and allowed traditional colors to blend with fabrics, making sunset shades acceptable for talls' dresses, and earth tones a welcome addition for the dresses of shorts.

"Such a beautiful color." Miles pointed at my chosen silk fabric.

He stood behind me, holding the radio and observing me with interest. He flipped through the channels, searching for a song that pleased him. As soon as he settled on a channel for more than a minute, he pressed the search button to move to the next one, and so on.

The other day, Rocky noted that the radio was a blessing for us as it was the only thing that could talk more than Miles. It was the only thing that could force him into silence; listening instead of chattering and rambling.

I was about to object to his constant switching of radio stations when the emergency news signal went on. An announcer's firm voice followed, announcing the death of our queen. Miles opened his mouth wide, shocked. He held the radio closer to me and pressed its side to increase the volume.

Both of us stood silent, rapt with attention. The announcer recounted details of the queen's illness and the rapidly deteriorating condition that claimed her life. My knees weakened, and I had a coughing fit. I stumbled to the nearest chair and steadied myself. I sat down and tried to process what had happened. I felt intense sadness despite having known about her poor health. Deep within, I had carried a handful of hope that the Sun would show us mercy with a miracle, heal her, and restore her to us as we knew her—strong, resilient, and robust, as she had always been.

"Oh, River of all Rivers, have mercy!" Miles began to pray.

"Oh, Sun! Have mercy!" I raised my hands to the sky and prayed.

We should have read the weather that day; we should have interpreted the signs of an impending disaster in the congestion of clouds in the sky, the sun hiding behind them, and the river raging. The gods were surely angry or saddened, preparing to receive her soul.

I was not in a good mood that morning. I had had a strange dream the night before; a dream I couldn't interpret. I didn't understand the emotions that accompanied me during it. I wondered if it was a vision, a dream, or a nightmare. In it, I felt like someone was squeezing my heart with a harsh grip.

In the dream I felt physically thin and frail, as if some curse had befallen me. I saw myself standing in a closed room alone with Tallan. Despite his presence, I felt queasy and uncomfortable. The curtains were closed, and the lighting was dim. I had a severe headache, and the room spun around me. It didn't stop spinning until I saw Tallan approaching me, extending his arms. He secured me by the waist, and lifted me with his strong, firm arms. My emaciated form offered no resistance as he raised me up into the sky. I screamed at him in a rage, demanding that he put me down.

In picking me up, Tallan had broken one of our most basic taboos. Once declared and confirmed in their height, shorts are never lifted from the ground until the day they die.

When I woke up, I felt anxious, afraid that the dream might signify my approaching end. But after calming down and realizing that it wasn't a vision of my death, I felt a strange sense of relief in my heart and some sort of happiness for feeling Tallan's arms embracing me with tenderness and affection. It was as if our roles had reversed. Tallan became the source of stability and strength, not me.

That confused me, and I couldn't find a logical interpretation for the dream. But if I wanted to be honest with myself, I had to admit that what I felt in it resembled the feeling I had when Tallan kissed me for the first time at my home. Despite feeling excited, I didn't understand my emotions, and I admit that I was afraid and tried to deny them. Perhaps it stirred something inside me that I was not ready to accept.

I shook these thoughts away and looked at Miles as he was still listening attentively to the announcer:

> As required by the constitution, the Prime Minister announces the start of the general population survey to search for the legitimate heir to the throne. Therefore, we request all adult citizens leave their work immediately and head to the city center, gathering by the Great River.

Immediately, I called out for Rocky and informed her of the tragedy. I asked her to hurry, tell her spouses, and bring them both to meet us at the corner of the street leading to the main market square.

After that, with Miles's help, I firmly closed all windows and doors. I left the fabrics I chose on the table so that I could continue working on the dress later.

11

He Is Barely a Cubit
and One Palm Tall

We put on our coats and scarves and headed toward the Big River. The weather that day was gloomy, marked by storms and strong winds. I knew I shouldn't walk with Miles on the same path because we were not family members and had no official bond. We should split up, with him taking the blue path on the right designated for talls, and me taking the green path on the left—the one for shorts. But given the strangeness of the day, I didn't think those conventions would matter.

We walked side by side in the middle lane reserved for couples and families, the one blending green and blue squares. The rain was falling in sheets and we had only one umbrella; the one Miles had been smart enough to bring with him this morning on his way to work. My umbrella had gotten snagged on a nail a few days ago and I hadn't yet been able to buy a new one.

Every single path was crowded with people responding to the news of the queen's death. I realized then that I'd never seen so many talls and shorts together, all of us intermingling as we pushed forward. With the increasing crowd and the rush of the masses, I began to worry about Miles. I feared he might get lost in the crowd and be hurt in the commotion. I held his arm firmly as we moved along. I wanted to protect him regardless of whether my actions made him uncomfortable. My priority was our safety. For his part, Miles didn't seem to register anything out of the ordinary. He held my hand comfortably, almost as if we were partners. We huddled together and walked toward the river, sharing Miles's umbrella.

Fortunately, the rain eased a few minutes after we arrived at the main market square behind the city's temple. We had just arrived at a momentous gathering: history in the making. We joined the enormous crowd gathering there, flowing in from all the streets connected to the square. I also noticed a significant security presence in the area to organize and protect the crowd and to separate talls from shorts.

The team of shortpolice worked swiftly to separate everyone by their appropriate height. The tallpolice lined up on the other side of the river to receive talls and organize them in rows. The pressure from the people behind us pushed us forward toward the guards, but I didn't want to leave Miles alone during the queen's cremation ceremony before Rocky and her spouses arrived. I needed to have Rocky with me during this difficult moment.

I scanned the crowd, looking for Rocky. I was surprised to realize that the person I was truly hoping to see was Tallan. My heart fluttered momentarily when I saw him smiling at me from among a group of shorts standing close by. I almost stepped toward them to greet him, but after a second look, I realized it wasn't him.

My heart gave another lurch when I thought I saw him among a group of talls, eagerly gesturing to me. I raised my hand in acknowledgment but, once again, realized it wasn't him. I clenched my hand and put it down. There was no denying it. I was looking for Tallan, not for Rocky.

I wondered whether he was present among the masses or not. If he were here, how would he choose to appear? Would he be a tall or a short today? Either way, would he disguise himself well enough to obscure his middling height? I was becoming worried.

"Can you see Rocky?" I called out to Miles. I hoped his height would give him a broader view. The noise of the crowd drowned me out.

"What did you say?" he called back.

I tried to raise my voice, but another coughing fit overcame me. I wondered if I had caught a cold or had been weakened by the bad weather.

"Are you okay?"

I nodded my head to reassure him. Eventually, the coughing fit passed and raised my voice again to repeat the question, "Rocky, Rocky, do you see her?"

"Yes, there she is."

I peered through the crowd, but I still couldn't see her. He grabbed my hand and pulled me forward into an open space in the mob. There they were: Rocky and her two spouses Ray and Pole. We approached them and I waved to them from a distance while Ray and Pole approached Miles, hugging and kissing him.

"How are you, Ray?" I asked her first, as she was Rocky's first and older spouse.

She shook her head and answered me with her usual coldness, "I'm fine."

Then, I turned to Rocky's second spouse, Pole. "And how are you, Pole, and how is the new baby?"

He smiled with joy, and I felt his excitement as he told me about the beauty of the baby born to Rocky a few months ago. How fast he was growing and changing every day. He quickly opened the cloth bag tied around his waist and took out a small box containing a recent photo of the baby. He handed it to me, pointing to the baby's eyes and his bulbous nose, just like his mother's.

"What a beautiful face!" I said. "Look at his chubby cheeks! How did he grow so fast?"

"Come with us after the ceremony to see him; you haven't visited us in weeks," Pole invited. "I'll cook your favorite dish, stuffed grape leaves."

Though I loved him and Rocky and stuffed grape leaves, I felt uncomfortable at their home because of Ray's presence. We didn't get along. I was not fond of her arrogance and didn't appreciate her moodiness and irritability. I couldn't understand why Rocky married her, even though I had been the one that asked for her hand in marriage for Rocky. Perhaps she was still angry with me because I had done the same with Pole. I wasn't the one who convinced Rocky to marry again, but I didn't refuse her request to lead the marriage proposal too, knowing well her need for children that she couldn't have from her marriage to Ray. Moreover, it was natural, even expected, for a short to remarry if their first spouse was of the same biological sex, when they married a tall of the opposite biological sex in their second marriage. Having children was socially desirable, despite some special cases where the short could settle with one spouse and sacrifice having children or desire two spouses of the same biological sex without caring about procreation.

I almost made up an excuse about work and declined the invitation, especially since I sensed Ray's cold stare as she remained silent and didn't respond. However, Rocky noticed my hesitation and quickly encouraged me, "Come and spend the evening with us. It's not a working day."

I looked at Miles, waiting for his opinion. His presence would ease any tension between me and Ray. He didn't object.

Afterward, I pointed to the shortpolice approaching us and urged the three talls to hasten and join the line of talls. I pulled and hurriedly led Rocky toward the shorts' line.

Once we were far from them, I asked Rocky, "What's wrong with Ray? She seems to be in a bad mood today."

"As usual, she had a minor argument with Pole this morning."

"Is she still jealous of the child?"

"She's jealous of everything now. She imagines things all the time. I'll tell you what happened later; she went too far this time," Rocky said as we approached the gathering of shorts.

I stood behind her in the line, waiting for the shortpolice to allow us entry into our designated area. I glanced toward the opposite side where Miles stood with Ray and

Pole. I saw Miles and Ray talking, and to my surprise, Ray was laughing heartily. It seemed her mood had changed the moment they moved away from me. Perhaps Miles had complimented her outfit and brightened her mood, as it was customary for talls to exaggerate their flattery when they met. Ray was always elegant. Indeed, she was extremely elegant; it was the primary quality that set her apart from Pole. Despite Pole's height advantage over Ray, she knew how to style herself to appear taller. She knew how to walk with a grace that few talls mastered. She seemed to move with the lightness of a slender giraffe and the head of an arrogant peacock, despite her round nose and thick lips, features that would have been more appropriate for someone short. Her elegance overshadowed her flaws and she captivated everyone she met.

The shortpolice began opening the lanes for the different height categories:

- The first row was for the shortest among us, the dwarves. They usually governed the country as members of the ruling council and ministers. Their height did not exceed three cubits and one palm.
- The second row was for shorts whose height was between three cubits and one palm and three cubits and three palms.
- The third row, to which Rocky and I belonged, extended from three cubits and three palms to three cubits and six palms.

In addition to these three categories, there was a special category for the sacred Royals who are extremely short, not exceeding two cubits' height. They were allocated golden seats in the elevated area of the bridge connecting the two banks. Today, the new ruler would be chosen from this category.

On the opposite side of the river, talls were grouped without being divided based on height, as it was not deemed essential. However, the first row was reserved for the spouses of the Royals and other dignitaries of the shorts community as a sign of respect. Talls, especially spouses of important personalities, were expected to show their national identity to affirm their status.

Once everyone had assembled in their designated rows, the Royal Guard's band began playing the Royal Anthem. A group of short, very obese soldiers carried the casket of the late queen and moved to the center of the bridge to a point exactly halfway between the banks. They headed toward the pyre of firewood that had been prepared, and placed the casket beside it. There, it was met by the Sun Temple's priestess who would lead the queen's cremation and complete the coronation of the new ruler.

Her presence was awe-inspiring not only because of her compact, powerful physique, but also because of the golden circle surrounding her head. Long golden rays extended from it, making it look like a glowing sun. Her ability to carry this immense golden circle entangled with her long white hair was a marvel, especially given the strong winds. I stared, wondering how it remained firmly in place. It was as if she embodied the human form of the Sun Goddess on earth. With her white robe, subtly tinged with yellow, and her monumental train, it seemed like her body hovered there in the stormy sky; the Sun Goddess reigning from above.

She stood proudly on the elevated platform in front of the pyre, holding her golden rod with a small disk shaped like a sun at its tip. She began reciting verses about death in a resonant voice that echoed through the loudspeakers, reaching us all. When her chanting finished, she took a torch from an attendant and carefully lit the firewood. Flames ignited, and they rose so high I was certain they touched the sky.

After a few minutes of hushed silence, the fire subsided, leaving only the sacred ashes of the queen's body inside the casket. The Royal Guard approached and gathered what remained of it before the wind carried it away. They placed it in a sacred vessel and handed it to the esteemed priestess, who carried it with dignity and approached the edge of the bridge, scattering it into the Great River.

"Indeed, this is our life. We live under the great Sun's light, and we return to it after our death through our sacred River," Rocky whispered to me, and I hugged her, feeling the weight of the scene and the mournful wails coming from the talls on the other side of the river.

Everyone settled as the Royal Guard's band played the Royal Anthem again, this time with a more powerful rhythm. The time had come to choose the queen's legitimate successor; the next ruler of our country. The four dwarf Royals stood on the platform alongside the Chief of the Royal Guard and the Army Commander, preparing for the final stage of the coronation. According to both tradition and the constitution, the choice of the successor was based on height. Every year, a census was conducted to record the heights of the adults; those eligible were invited to join the Council of Royals, the Council of Dignitaries, or the Ministerial Team. The shortest short in the entire country was considered the most sacred and, therefore, divinely chosen to rule.

A team from the army stepped forward to measure the height of each Royal nominated for the throne and record it on a large board behind the platform. Their heights were quite close, but the shortest among them was Prince Knuckle, whose height did not exceed one cubit and one palm. While this was acceptable, it was less promising than the late queen, whose height was one cubit and three fingers.

Before the new king's inauguration, the Army Commander had to address the general public to confirm that the chosen king was, in fact, the shortest short in the country. Three times he called out, asking if anyone knew of anyone shorter than Knuckle. If anyone shorter was discovered, they must come forward to assume the divine responsibility of ruling the nation.

The Army Commander repeated the question, following the laws laid down in the constitution, and waited for a minute of silence to pass. The entire crowd waited, holding their breath. In the end the Commander declared Knuckle as the rightful and divine king, regent of the entire nation.

The Royal Anthem played for the third time, and fireworks lit up the sky, filling the atmosphere with joy and celebration for the beginning of a new era.

12

Shorts Are from Jupiter, and Talls Are from Neptune

Neither Rocky nor Miles were happy with the choice of the new king. Rocky was pessimistic because he wasn't as short as the previous queen, and Miles seemed annoyed, grumbling that the traditional way of succession had become outdated. As for Ray, she didn't care much, as her private matters were more important than anything else. However, she decided to join them in their gloomy mood when we arrived at Rocky's place. It wasn't the new king or how he was chosen that annoyed Ray; it was me.

As for Pole, he wasn't interested in public affairs anymore, as his life revolved around taking care of his little child. He hurried to collect the child from the neighbors' house, where they had left him under the care of their teenage children until our return. When Pole appeared at the door, he was holding the child between his hands as if it were a doll, arms extended, offering it to me.

I moved toward him, eager to meet him, and gasped again, just like I did when I first saw his photo a few hours ago. I didn't expect him to be this adorable. "Oh, what a beautiful chubby baby he is!" I exclaimed in amazement. "What a gorgeous chubby baby he is!"

I raised my fingers and drew a circle in the air to protect him and bless him. I couldn't help but pinch his rounded cheeks. I pressed them as if I were pressing a rubber ball, not realizing the strength of my fingers until his face changed, and he burst into tears.

Ray gave me a sharp look, blaming me for my foolishness, and took the baby from Pole, who seemed unsure how to handle his crying. She hugged the baby and walked him around the house until he calmed down. After that, she sat next to Miles in the corner of the room and kept herself busy talking to him while rocking the baby.

Pole excused himself and went to the kitchen to prepare the food. Shortly after, Rocky went to the bathroom. I was left alone on the couch, sitting some distance away from Ray and Miles.

To my good fortune, I found a book lying on the table before me and picked it up idly. I glanced, then flipped it over to read the title. In large letters, the book proclaimed:

Shorts Are from Jupiter
(written in green)
Talls Are from Neptune
(written in blue)

It was a book I had heard about and wanted to read. I, like many others, was interested in what this self-proclaimed expert in marital relationships had to say. The book's main idea was to explain and attribute the deep psychological differences between shorts and talls—differences that could lead to emotional difficulties in their relationships. The author believed that we could avoid these difficulties if we understood and dealt with them properly.

I examined the back cover and found a large quote:

"The most famous book published about marital relationships. A global phenomenon."

It was true; other than myself, I didn't know anyone who hadn't read it yet. The book's summary followed:

> *Shorts Are from Jupiter and Talls Are from Neptune* has helped millions of couples correct the course of their marital relationships. This book is considered one of the most important books of our era. It clarifies the differences between shorts and talls, explaining how each type can and should express their needs in a way that doesn't lead to conflicts.

The book's title highlighted the significant differences between the two human types as if they were created on two planets: Jupiter for shorts, due to its large size, and Neptune for talls, due to its distance from the sun.

The back cover continued, making the following claims:

> Dear reader, *Shorts Are from Jupiter and Talls Are from Neptune* will show you how to:
> (1)
> Build lasting, loving short-tall relationships.
> (2)
> Learn how to read moods and respond effectively.

(3)

Get what you need without seeming to nag or bully.

(4)

Communicate difficult feelings and emotions.

(5)

Avoid the pain of argument.

(6)

Understand your spouse, colleagues,
or friends better than ever before.

I had finished reading the back cover just as Rocky returned from the bathroom. She ordered Ray to hurry and help Pole finish preparing dinner. She also asked Ray to make coffee for us and to fetch us some nuts. And that's what she did. Ray heard Rocky's instructions, ended her conversation with Miles quickly, and got up, annoyed. She approached Rocky, handed the baby to her, and gave me a sharp look, warning me not to disturb him again. After that, she rushed to the kitchen.

I held up the book in my hands and asked, "Which of you has read this book?"

As far as I knew, Rocky didn't enjoy reading.

Pole answered excitedly as he entered the reception room, carrying the coffee tray he had prepared, "It's a fantastic book. I read it all in one sitting!"

He sat on the couch and placed the tray in his lap. He filled our cups with coffee. "I liked how the author sheds light on the close relationship between blood pressure levels and the psychological state. He explains how high or low blood pressure affects a person's mood, behavior, and interaction with their surroundings."

He handed me a coffee cup. "According to the author, this is directly related to the person's height. High blood pressure clearly explains the shorts' moodiness and aggressiveness."

Rocky nodded in agreement.

I, too, felt some logic in his words. Earth and fire are associated with shorts, while water and air are associated with talls. Also, talls' responsibility of understanding and dealing with us according to our fiery nature was a reasonable suggestion. But Pole's words didn't convince Miles. As usual, he quickly objected, "But moodiness, nervousness, and aggressiveness are not exclusive to shorts. I know talls who are moodier than any short I've ever met."

I almost jumped from my seat and wanted to shout Ray's name as an example to support Miles's point, but I controlled myself.

Pole responded, "You are talking about specific cases. The book speaks generally, building its conclusions on statistical studies. Much of the current scientific research confirms a direct and undeniable relationship between obesity, blood pressure, and psychological state. This is a reality we cannot deny."

I admired Pole's composure and self-assurance but knew his words would never convince Miles. I wondered about Tallan and his neither-nor height. What is his blood pressure level? Is he moody, nervous like shorts, or calm and cool-headed like talls? He remained calm and composed and didn't move a bit when he saw me rushing to bring the gun!

"I think it's challenging to simplify human traits and summarize them this way," Miles objected. "There might be a correlation between obesity and blood pressure, but we also know that there are many other elements that affect blood pressure such as everyday life, genetics, medicine, smoking, etc. Moreover, blood pressure isn't the sole source of a person's emotional state. There are plenty of other factors that can lead to nervousness or make us angry and aggressive."

"You are still talking about special cases," Rocky said. Her tone was diplomatic, trying to avoid another endless argument. Pole nodded in agreement, and before Miles could object, offered him a cup of herbal tea.

"Can I have coffee?"

Pole apologized and hurried to get him a cup of coffee. Rocky's face turned red, but she didn't say anything.

"Even in general," Miles continued, responding to Rocky's words, "if the author carefully examined the data he relied on to build his conclusions, he would find some extremely high blood pressure readings in shorts. These readings are considered health conditions today, requiring medical treatment to bring blood pressure down to normal levels. Without these exceptionally high blood pressure cases, there wouldn't be a significant difference in average blood pressure between talls and shorts."

When Pole returned, Miles took his coffee cup, sipped from it, and confidently stated, "I've read a recent book that exposes all the mistakes the author made and provides a detailed critique of the book. Everyone who read that book should read this one too."

Rocky's face flushed even more as she listened to Miles.

"The book acknowledges that we should pay attention to the direct correlation between excessive consumption of fatty and sugary foods and high blood pressure. We have witnessed the loss of some of our relatively young rulers due to heart attacks and clogged arteries caused by high blood pressure resulting from obesity."

I knew that Miles's rhetoric provoked Rocky since she strongly rejected this narrative, seeing it as a direct attack on shorts' identity. I quickly changed the subject and joked while holding my belly, shaking it with pride, "Is there anything more beautiful than obesity? Where's the food, Pole? My stomach can't tolerate hunger."

I pointed at the three talls and accused them, "I know you conspire against Rocky and me because of our obesity."

"It will be ready in five minutes," Pole reassured me with a laugh before inviting Miles and Ray to enter the kitchen to finish preparing the meal. After that, I looked at Rocky, who seemed upset. I approached her, placed my hand on hers, and asked her not to focus on what Miles said. He was simply young and impulsive. She nodded in agreement but surprised me by admitting that her annoyance was not at Miles but her pessimism about the new king's rule.

I couldn't help but express my astonishment and disapproval of her backward thinking, "Are you pessimistic because the new king is taller than the previous one? I can't believe you still hold such retrogressive ideas!"

She didn't have a convincing response for me. She admitted, "Yes, I feel pessimistic and don't need to justify it. Our history shows that some of the best periods of our country's prosperity were under the rule of the shortest rulers."

"Rocky!" I exclaimed, adding, "That was in the past. Most countries today are not governed by shorts. Some tall rulers have ruled other countries for decades, and their countries are progressing and advancing faster than us. Some of their countries are more successful than we are."

"It doesn't matter to me what others do. We have a cultural uniqueness that doesn't exist anywhere else in the world," she argued, passion in her eyes.

Miles returned from the kitchen and, unable to hold back his opinion, interjected. "Why do we insist on clinging to height as the sole measure for choosing our rulers? A capable ruler needs a variety of experiences and skills. Why settle for short stature? Why couldn't there be a tall ruler? Isn't it time for a change?"

13

Every System in the Universe Has a Short at Its Center and a Tall Revolving around Its Axis

Tallan had disappeared. Several nights had passed without him knocking on my door. As each night went by, my longing for him and my concern grew. I had hoped he would visit me the night following his last visit, but I didn't expect him to come because it was the night of the queen's death and the new king's coronation. I hadn't worried about his absence the following nights, although I was eager to see him.

Now I was looking for a way to justify his absence. I wondered if he distanced himself because of something I said or did. Did he not like my kisses? Did I misread his desires? That was possible and I had to admit that, at times, my emotional intelligence was limited. Perhaps he changed his mind and no longer needed the outfit he planned to wear for the family wedding. Or maybe the wedding was postponed and he didn't have to rush for the dress? Or could it have been canceled altogether?

But shouldn't he have come and apologized, letting me know what happened? He is a person of noble origins and high morals.

I nearly lost my mind while analyzing all the scenarios that could explain his disappearance. I even checked with acquaintances through Miles that the wedding wasn't canceled and was indeed on schedule. From the third night onward, I started going to the city center early in the morning, spending the daylight hours among fabric shops, hoping to run into him. I stayed awake late into the night, listening carefully for any knocking on the door, waiting for him.

After ten days, as my daily market tour ended, I felt hungry. I decided to sit in one of the restaurants near the Great River and have lunch. It was there that I wandered in thought. I say "wandered in thought" as if he hadn't occupied my mind before. I had dedicated myself to searching for a way to communicate with him. While eating at the restaurant's courtyard, overlooking the river, I could see grand luxurious houses on the other riverbank at the top of the hill. I remembered Tallan telling me his family's name during his first visit. So, it immediately occurred to me that if he told the truth, one of those houses must belong to his family. Perhaps he still lived there, not having moved to the bachelor talls' buildings surrounding it after his mother's death as I had previously assumed.

I didn't feel like going home that day. The weather was unusually sunny for spring and I felt a sense of solitude. I wasn't in the mood for sewing, designing, or receiving any of my customers. I decided to cross the bridge and walk to the opposite side to explore new places in the city that were not part of my usual trips. I let my feet lead me, hoping they would guide me to his doorstep as his had led him to me. I believed in destiny and I felt that the desire that arose within me wouldn't have been so intense if it didn't mean anything. I was lost in my thoughts but searched the faces of passersby around me, looking for any sign that could explain his disappearance from my life.

I walked on the lane designated for shorts, observing young children in their innocent yellow clothes playfully hopping around their parents in the family lane. I looked to the far left, hoping to see Tallan crossing the narrow talls' path, but it was empty. On my right, I enjoyed the sight of pine trees with their short branches stretching along the shorts' path. In a beautiful symmetry I saw, on the other side of the bridge, to the left of the talls' path, tall cypress trees with their tapered tops towering above us.

I had imagined Tallan crossing this bridge on his way to me, assuring myself that he must have walked along the talls' path during his first visit. After a moment of thought and remembering his appearance on his subsequent visit, I shook my head and smiled, realizing that my feet were treading the same path that he might have taken toward me. I then realized I was searching for him on the talls' path, even though he could have taken any of the three paths: He could have been accompanied by family, or with a spouse who differed in height, or disguised as a short.

For the first time in my life, I felt the constraint of these lines. For the first time, the voices opposing the division of public spaces according to social types felt right to me! What nonsense led us to divide public roads based on who is tall and who is short? Was it truly to protect our talls from the barbarism of shorts like me? Shouldn't we have established civilized boundaries that emphasize our humanity and create safe spaces for everyone, regardless of height? Why insist on such a binary perpetuating the idea that shorts are aggressors and talls are victims? Do we surrender to the belief that our animalistic side, desires, and instincts can only be civilized through dividing and defining spaces between us?

If only this were limited to these paths, I sighed. I wandered in my thoughts, thinking about our world built entirely on the sanctity of height—the sanctity of measuring the horizontal distance between two points.

Their connection forms a line.

Their meeting forms the shortest line, a point.

The point from which the world exploded.

Our shortness represents the point of the greatest explosion, the big bang.

The starting point for the lines of our time and space.

The lines that represent our tallness.

Two types of energy govern our world, balanced due to the harmony of shorts' and talls' energies. These two energies manifest in everything in nature. From the smallest mass of an atom, reflecting shorts' strength, to the paths of electrons, expressing the extension of talls, and to the largest cosmic masses in solar systems and the paths of their planets orbiting around their stars. Every system in the universe has a short at its center and a tall rotating around its axis.

In all their varieties, our trees are divided into short and tall trees. In nature, you find them drawn according to a sacred natural code. You see short plants accompanying dense grass and giant cedars, displaying a natural harmony reflecting the cosmic state.

Our animals are classified into two types. They are categorized as animals with short characteristics and others with tall characteristics. There are robust, sturdy animals and slender, elegant ones. There are ground-bound reptiles, friendly to shorts, and sky-bound birds, allies of the talls. Then there is the sacred category, which crosses the boundaries and combines characteristics of both types, like slender, long-bodied snakes sticking to the ground.

I stopped my musings as I reached the opposite bank of the river. For a moment, I drifted in thought, recalling the logical paradox that had manifested before me. Sacred snakes? A reality we live in. We revere animals that combine the qualities of both of us, but we condemn individuals who do the same. Isn't that strange? Why do we elevate the value of the snake while denying Tallan's right to exist? We revere the snake; why don't we also revere Tallan and others like him?

I dismissed the thought from my head, fearing to indulge in blasphemy. I hesitated to continue my journey. To my right, in an area not yet reached by urban design, amid the randomness of trees and the intertwining of their branches, I caught sight of a person emerging from an uneven sandy path.

I thought they were short, with a hunched back and a natural hump on the top of it, or at least that's how I wanted to see them! Similar to Tallan. Or were they like that? I didn't know.

I hastened to approach them to make sure they weren't Tallan. Unfortunately, they disappeared before I could discern their features. I couldn't determine which way they went, and curiosity led me to venture into that dim path between the shadows of the trees to see where it led. "It won't lead to Tallan's house," I told myself. I tried to think logically, not wanting to waste my time as I still needed to reach the top of the hill and search among its grand houses.

I continued my journey toward my destination. I climbed the winding half-circle path, ascending the few steps that separated me from the area it led to, getting closer to the high houses, anxiously wanting to read the name of each house. I wasn't disappointed when I reached the top of the hill, as I found what I was looking for.

Right there before me stood the Skys' palace.

In my imagination, I heard echoes of Tallan's childish laughter resonating in my heart. I saw him in his yellow attire playing in the vast gardens of the palace. He was as innocent as a child chasing a dog running after a ball. He must have been a carefree child, unaware that the world would reject him someday.

I approached the gate and stood between the gates designated for talls and those designated for shorts as I caught the fragrant scent of jasmine, filling my lungs, conjuring up the sight of Tallan when he surprised me with a bouquet of jasmine.

Oh, how I miss you, Tallan!

I sighed.

For a moment, I hesitated before ringing the bell. How could I justify my presence here? What if one of the short family members opened the gate? How could I explain my relationship with Tallan? Wasn't his visit to me meant to be secret, even from his family?

My longing for him outweighed my fear, so I extended my finger and pressed the bell in the middle between the tall and short gates, hoping I'd be lucky and he would open the door. After a minute, I heard light footsteps, and my heart pounded to the sound. I felt a sense of relief as I heard someone approaching the tall-gate, and I watched as the gate opened quietly.

One of the maids appeared, standing beside the gate cautiously, wondering why I was there. Her skin color and accent revealed that she was foreign. I struggled to communicate with her but I managed to ask her about Tallan. She understood my question but denied any knowledge of him, assuring me, stuttering, that there was no resident of that palace whose name was Tallan.

She closed the gate in my face after confirming that this was not the destination I was searching for.

14

What the Hell Did I Walk into

I was puzzled as I marched down the hill, wondering what had happened. I was at the front step of Tallan's family home and did not find him there. The maid's denial of knowing him left me wondering. Was she lying to me? Or was he the one lying?

I couldn't imagine him being deceitful. He seemed genuine when he first visited me. I swear he sounded genuine; it was his soul's purity that attracted me to him. Moreover, I couldn't find a reason for him to lie after confessing something tragic about his family. The maid's denial seemed genuine as well, despite her haste in dismissing me. Perhaps my surprise visit had upset her? Or maybe she was dealing with a family problem that forced her to deny Tallan's existence? If that were true, it would be very sad. I didn't know what to think!

My concern grew.

My heart was heavy and sad as I crossed the bridge home, when I noticed two talls walking toward that unpaved sandy path between the trees. They caught my attention as they were distinctly different and strikingly odd. Both were unusually tall and stout. I linked them in my head to the detested gluttonous talls who resembled shorts. Their confidence shook me as I saw them walking in their green robes like those worn by shorts. The fact that they wore their hair like shorts infuriated me. Although I heard about the gluttonous and their increasing numbers and peculiarities, I felt offended seeing them like that.

If Rocky were with me, she would have attacked them without hesitation, reprimanding them severely and probably assaulting them. But as I contemplated her re-action, I remembered how she screamed when she first saw Tallan. Before I got to know him, I felt the same way and wasn't sure about him. But I changed my mind and became more accepting, so I decided to ignore my fear and walked toward the strangers.

I stepped into the alley; the sun was almost down and the entrance was dim. Inside, it was lit by candles spaced out along the walls. From a distance, I heard loud music, whispers, laughter, and the clink of glasses. As I entered, I noticed it wasn't an abandoned passage. It had been re-vamped and refurbished with beautiful flowers on every corner.

The path led to a courtyard with a coffee place I had heard of, although I hadn't known where it was located. The ambiance felt weird. At first, it felt like a tourist spot, bustling with foreign visitors. It was a convenient excuse for the owner to turn it into a spot where talls and shorts could meet in public without strict boundaries. I found that delightful, being open-minded myself. However, as I approached the crowd and sat at a table, I spotted a cou-ple, a tall and a short, with lips locked in a passionate kiss.

When I looked intently at their foreheads, I was surprised that they were single, with no cross tattooed on their foreheads.

The waiter brought me the drinks menu and waited for my order. I looked at him and I felt something odd about his appearance. Despite being short with a normal build, his hair was light and cut so short that it didn't suit him. I was not too fond of shorts with almost-bald heads.

I thought about asking him about Tallan but I hesitated. Instead, I ordered a fruit juice and looked back at the lovebirds in front of me, but was distracted by another couple sitting to their right. This couple wasn't entwined in an intimate embrace or engaged in a romantic kiss; they huddled together closely, holding hands as if they were the protagonists of a love story.

My eyes widened as I realized they were both shorts!

I opened my mouth in amazement. Since when do same-height couples flaunt their romance in public? Have we lost our manners? Where the hell was I?

I stood up, intending to leave the place, but as I looked around, I felt like I was the stranger, not them. I thought of the young man with the hump who I had seen leaving the alley just hours ago. I wondered if this place provided a haven for Tallan and those who resembled him. I noticed several medium-height individuals who seemed comfortable and happy to be there. So, I decided to stay longer, hoping Tallan would show up.

To add to all the awkwardness, I was surprised to see someone I knew well enter the place as if he belonged there.

15

Doesn't She Have
the Right of Choice

Miles entered the place with a friend of his, a tall. He was buzzing around, chatting with everyone as if he knew them all. Although I knew he was talkative, I didn't expect him to have so many friends. It seemed he was a regular at this cafe. This made me wonder if he knew about Tallan.

"Hey, Miles!" I called out to him. He was surprised to see me. He quickly greeted me and approached with his friend, whom he introduced to me as Willow.

As they joined me, he eagerly asked me how I found my way to this place.

"I was wandering around the area when I spotted two strangers entering a pathway among the trees. Curiosity got the best of me, and I followed them, only to discover this beautiful place at the end of the path.

"And what about you? How did you come to know about this place?"

"I've known it for a while and love its ambiance. It's not like any other cafe in the city."

"It does seem different, but I find it somewhat strange." I didn't shy from expressing my discomfort with being in this place, yet I was cautious not to criticize it in front of him, especially after sensing his excitement and his friend's approval. Having known him for some time, I knew he wouldn't keep quiet and would argue with me for hours to convince me of the beauty of this place and that my discomfort was unjustified.

"Strange? What's strange about it?" he asked me with surprise, looking around the cafe calmly as if trying to show me that everyone around us appeared normal.

I didn't want to sound close-minded in front of him and his new friend, whom I had just met for the first time. I had no idea what she thought about this, so I tried to explain myself in the most neutral way possible. "I mean how people look here, they look different than the people you usually see in other places around the town."

I said that while observing a short passing among the tables in a graceful light walk that didn't fit her short stature. Her appearance provoked me, like the two heavily built talls I saw entering the pathway. Like them, she was bold with her choice of dress, wearing a blue robe that defies social norms. "Does she think she's a tall?" I said, pointing to her. "Have people lost their minds?!" I gasped as I observed her slender figure that contradicted her shortness, and her completely bald head that made her look like any other tall!

"No, she hasn't!" Miles answered me in a serious tone. He looked astonished, as if I had said something rude or inappropriate. "She feels like a tall and likes to behave as a tall, what's wrong with that?"

What's wrong with that?! I nearly repeated his question, appalled at his simple justification and acceptance of her unusual appearance as if it were a normal thing that I had no right to comment on.

"But this goes against reason and nature," I couldn't help myself. "I don't think she's taller than me. How can she delude herself with such illusions?"

I looked at her again and commented playfully, "Doesn't she have a height scale at home?"

"What contradicts what you're used to doesn't necessarily contradict nature," he responded with a defensive tone, and argued with me audaciously. "Moreover, the measurements of height are relative and vary from one society to another."

I didn't understand what he meant by saying that height is relative, and he didn't allow me to interrupt him.

"I believe she knows her height perfectly well," he said. Then, to add to my confusion, he added, "Perhaps she likes her short stature as it is, or she feels taller than she is."

"Or maybe she doesn't like her shortness and tries to deny it."

He then concluded, "All possibilities are valid. I don't know her, but all these options do not mean she doesn't have the right to walk like we talls do, dress the way we do, or shave her head completely like we do. Doesn't she have the right to choose what she finds suitable for herself?"

"She has complete freedom; I don't judge her here. On the other hand, I have the complete freedom to be astonished by her strange appearance," I defended myself. Trying to deal with the situation with an open mind, I suggested what I thought would be an appropriate solution for her case, "Why not consider surgery to lengthen her legs so she can achieve her desired height and her appearance won't be considered strange anymore?"

"She doesn't look strange to me!"

No one else would make that claim as strongly as Miles. He added with a tense tone, "You suggest surgery as if it were an easy matter! Do you know how much such operations cost? Do you realize how difficult they are and the amount of pain involved?"

He waited for my answer but when he saw my surprise at his reaction, he said calmly, "She might be one of those trans-height who are comfortable with their short stature but not with their weight. She may want to be tall, not in her height, but in her grace, softness, and behavior."

He reiterated the question, challenging me, "Why don't we accept her choices?"

"Frankly, I find it challenging to understand this category of people. I understand if someone of a certain height is attracted to someone of a similar height. Still, I don't understand the need to show off in public, assuming the features of the opposite type with no shame," I defended my point while showing that I accept what is rejected by most people in our society. But that wasn't enough to convince him. His eyes widened with even greater surprise, "So you are saying that you accept that an individual would go out of the norm as long as it is done in secret?

"Isn't that what we call hypocrisy?" he accused me. He didn't give me a chance to clarify my perspective. "And why do you assume that she is attracted to shorts?"

"Because she visually represents talls!" I explained my perspective after he provoked me, "I don't think there's any other reason driving her to act this way other than her desire to attract shorts to her!"

He laughed mockingly and added confidently, "Attracting shorts is not why she resembles talls. But to convince you of that, you need to allow me to explain the basic characteristics that constitute our social types."

16

There Are No Talls, Shorts, or Mediums—Just People of Different Heights

I didn't understand what he meant when he said "the basic characteristics that constitute our social types." He said it confidently, though then he tried to explain it to me as if he were a teacher, granting me the seat of a student even though I was twenty years older than him.

I let him finish without interruption. But as I write this story, I admit that he taught me a valuable lesson back then, leaving me bewildered, pondering this world I now see differently.

Observing people around me in the coffeehouse, I was lost in thought. I was still surprised by this strange mixture of different heights and weights when Miles explained the matter to me briefly.

"Height, as a biological trait, does not exist in only two specific forms."

It was apparent but I had not realized it. I saw the difference in the heights of the talls and that of the shorts, but unconsciously, I had categorized all the talls into one group and included all the shorts in another. And I, like others, found beauty in talls who are taller, and gave more value for shorts who are shorter. I also wrongly believed that all people of medium height were created similarly and that their state represents a biological defect or genetic deviation. I did not know that their height varied and that some were closer in height to talls while others were closer to shorts.

Who imposed these height boundaries upon us? When were they set?

Miles didn't have the answer, but he confirmed that these height boundaries are illusory, saying that nature does not have a scalpel to cut human traits and classify them to satisfy our whims.

I realized that day that there are no talls, shorts, or mediums, just people of different heights. And I was pleased to conclude that. But Miles did not stop there; he added another statement that confused me.

"Height as a biological trait is different from height as a social type."

He explained that the former is a biological trait that varies among humans, but the latter is a social classification of this trait: a classification that gives preference to one form over the other and assigns other attributes to amplify the distinction between individuals.

"Talls are known not only for their height but by a mixture of other added traits." I remember what he said, and I remember that I did not argue with him, for it was true and clear to me. A tall must be slim, bald, and weak-bodied, often sensitive with a soft voice. In contrast, a short must be stout, strong, with thick hair, and less emotional—as if human traits were dissected and distributed according to height to create two opposing human types.

I had previously believed that these traits come combined in one package as a gift from the gods. It was obvious that talls are slimmer because the food they eat is distributed over a larger mass. It's natural for shorts to have thicker hair, as the strength of hair is associated with body strength and physical health.

"But what if these traits are not linked in reality?" Miles asked me to add to my confusion. "What if being slim is not related to height? Or if the abundance of hair has no relation to body health?

"And what if we realized that talls are slim because of social habits, not their biological genes?"

I did not know how to answer all those questions, because everyone around me outside the space of this coffeehouse was embodying the links between these traits in one way or another. I only came across these traits shown in contrast in very few special cases. Is our inherited culture possibly so strong as to obscure all this existing diversity? Or was Miles exaggerating in his proposition? Or are those traits not entirely independent but often come together, as our cultural, intellectual, and religious heritage asserts?

What he was saying was puzzling and new to me. It was hard to absorb all that at once. So, I asked him to wait until I could go to the bathroom to relieve myself.

I returned afterward, ordered a cup of strong coffee, and asked him to continue.

17

How One Feels about Their Height Is Relative

He pointed to an important aspect that reveals the cultural differences between our society and other societies in applying the social attributes of height.

"What we perceive suitable for talls and what we impose as a duty on shorts is not an absolute reality."

I realized this through my travels and interactions with foreigners. For instance, some societies assign white for talls' clothes and brown for shorts' clothes, instead of the blue and green garments we wear. I remembered the Eastern fashion magazines I got every month as I started my career as a tailor. It was surprising to see the colors used. But they became normal over the years when I grew up and realized the difference in traditional dresses and their diversity across cultures. However, Miles did not focus just on the biological and societal dimensions of height, but also added the individual's self-perception of their characteristics and what this perception entails. How can individuals be aware of their diverse features, and how can they accept, reject, or come to terms with them?

"The individual's sense of their height might not necessarily correspond with the actual measurement of that height."

What he said confused me even more.

He further explained that an individual's perception of their height is relative. He gave an example of how the tallest sibling in a family of shorts might feel. They usually perceive themselves as taller than they are because their siblings describe them as "the tall among us." Similarly, the shortest among a group of tall siblings might feel that they are short, even if they are quite tall.

Miles referred to the girl whom I previously ridiculed, reaffirming that she might feel taller than how we perceive her, or she might be aware of her biological height as it is but finds her other qualities closer to the opposite social type.

Before I could comment on what he said, he clarified that feeling tall doesn't necessarily correlate with to whom she's attracted to. He explained that in our culture, we tend to give significance to our sexual desires and assume it is the primary force behind one's appearance and behavior.

And that was the most shocking thing he said that night.

18

The One Type
No One Acknowledges

Miles added, "The attraction toward others is independent of one's biological height and social type. It is not right to categorize it or assume it is distributed automatically per one's height."

He meant to say that the prevalent belief that talls are only attracted to shorts and vice versa is incorrect. "That girl might be attracted to shorts, talls, or both. We can't know for sure unless we ask her. And she might not even be sure herself," he explained.

"The attraction toward a specific height is a spectrum just like biological height itself."

Although he said it is a spectrum, he went on to categorize one's preference toward a certain height in the same way we categorize biological height:

1. Opposite-height-lovers: those attracted to the individuals' opposite in height. They make up the dominant and only accepted category for us.
2. Same-height-lovers: those attracted to individuals of the same height; a category we don't

acknowledge in our society and don't generally accept, but it's becoming more accepted in other societies.

3. Lovers-of-both-heights: those who love both talls and shorts regardless of height; we don't accept the fact that they exist.

And finally, the category that no one acknowledges—those we rarely pay attention to—those who are attracted to mediums; i.e., individuals of medium height.

It felt that he knew my secret when he mentioned the last category, as if he knew the depth of my attraction to Tallan.

In reality, he wasn't aware of that yet.

He proceeded to explain that many factors influence one's attraction and desire toward another individual. The most significant factor might be height, but sex, skin color, ethnicity, and other traits also play essential roles.

This was logical for me. While I was usually attracted to talls, I preferred talls who are males. This was the main reason for the failure of my previous relationship. Despite her height and slenderness, I wasn't attracted to my ex's body. It was Tallan's genitalia that I liked. It may have overshadowed the fact of him being a medium.

19

I Realized I Was No Longer
a Stranger to the Place

After detailing the essential traits in their various dimensions, he asked the waiter for paper and a pen. He concluded by explaining that when combined, these varied and graded traits produce multiple forms of humans. However, being a society that loves categorizing and classifying people, we have created two socially accepted molds. Anything outside of them is rejected and demonized.

He began drawing different human forms from that set of traits on the paper. One of the molds caught my attention, and I found myself in it. My attraction to Tallan was strange and not socially welcomed, same as his average height. But as a short, I possessed certain advantages regarding the acceptance of my choice of sexual partners as long as it didn't directly conflict with my role in society.

That day, I realized that I no longer felt out of place. I understood that I was just like them—different, just like that short who considered herself to be tall. The idea of a relationship between a fellow short and a medium like

Tallan is repulsive to many. And being a chubby short with long hair doesn't give me the right to judge others.

However, his mention of biological sex that day as an important factor among other factors of attraction between people triggered me to think and paved the way for a revolutionary idea. It dominated my thoughts and established the grounds of a hypothetical world that could be more suitable for me and for Tallan.

A world where people are divided by their sex, not their height.

20

How Can I Not Support Someone I Consider Part of My Family

I woke up early, waiting for Miles with bated breath as dawn broke. After firmly holding onto the words he told me yesterday and witnessing his persistent defense of those who are different, I realized he wouldn't judge me if I confided in him about my relationship with Tallan. He wouldn't look down on me or be surprised by my attachment to him, as Rocky did when I confided in her. I wanted to ask him if he knew about Tallan's sudden disappearance and the reason for his absence.

I looked for an opportunity to interact with him after I sent Rocky to get my things from the market. I eagerly waited for him when he entered the fabric room holding the morning coffee he prepared for me. Unlike his usual self, he was not cheerful and chatty. He greeted me with a barely audible voice, handing me a trembling cup of coffee.

I took the cup from him and sipped it while preparing myself to ask the question that was on my mind: Do you know someone named Tallan?

But before I could say a word, I noticed he was significantly tense. I changed course to check if he was okay. "Miles, you seem worried today. What's wrong?"

"Nothing, nothing," he said, trying to deny what he was going through. The tremor in his bones made it impossible to ignore his feelings. I helped him sit down, sensing his difficulty in speaking, and went to the kitchen to get him a glass of water to calm him. I gave him the water to drink. I put my hand on his shoulder, urging him to relax before I asked him again, "Miles, tell me, what's wrong? Why are you trembling like this?"

He looked at me with fearful eyes, hesitant to reveal what was on his mind. His silence was enough to tell me that what he was hiding was serious.

"What's the matter, cat got your tongue?" I teased, trying to lighten the mood. I rested my hand on his shoulder to reassure him and whispered, "Tell me, don't be afraid."

"Do you remember my friend you met yesterday at the cafe?" he asked, a look of fear in his eyes.

"Yes, of course, I remember her. What about her?"

He paused again, stood up, and began pacing the room, trying to muster courage, then said, "After you left the cafe, we were alone and started talking. She had previously told me she wanted to discuss something important but I didn't expect what she said."

"What did she say? What did she tell you?" I lost patience.

"She told me she's pregnant!"

"Pregnant!"

His revelation took me aback. I didn't know her that well. She seemed to be roughly the same age as Miles, and it was clear from the vertical line on her forehead that she wasn't married yet, so that means she got pregnant from an extramarital sexual relationship. Being a tall, her pregnancy would be frowned upon if she were married, but the implications are severe if she were unmarried.

"Whoa!"

I shot a question at him in amazement, thinking I had the solution to her problem, "Who is the short she got pregnant with? She should marry him immediately so he can stand by her and take responsibility for the pregnancy."

He bit his lip and shook his head. "She can't marry him."

"Why not? Is he a stranger to the city and her family won't accept him?" I asked, puzzled.

"No."

"Does he follow a different religion?" I inquired further.

"No, that's not the issue,"

I was about to go through all the obvious questions about why she couldn't marry the short who got her pregnant, but I composed myself and asked, "What's preventing her from marrying him?"

He shocked me when he said, "She's pregnant by a tall, a tall like her!"

At that moment, I understood his concern for her. His friend had gotten herself into a huge predicament that might cost her her life. Extramarital relationships were taboo and usually resulted in punishment if discovered. Now suppose the relationship was considered deviant, as in the case of two individuals of the same height. In that case, the public perceived it as even more dangerous, especially if it led to the birth of a child, who would be considered cursed before he saw the light of day. In this case, the official law stipulated the removal of the child from both parents, with both serving a prison sentence of no less than ten years. However, the societal law that most families abided by would lead to the killing of both individuals.

Before I could process what he said, I saw him break down before me, tearfully confessing that he was the father.

I stood there, shocked and puzzled, as if struck by thunder, shaking in my place. This was the first time I heard him speak so openly about his deviant same-height attraction. Even though I prided myself for being different from others, for being more accepting and tolerant toward this group of people, his confession shook me to the bones.

For a moment, I remembered Tallan. I recalled when he knocked on my door asking for my assistance, openly and honestly confessing his height. I remembered his hesitation when I asked him to take off his shoes, how his eyes filled with many emotions that softened my heart. How his story affected me, and how I fell in love with him. At that time, I thought I could keep our relationship professional, but I failed. And here was Miles, who I loved dearly, almost like a younger brother or a young son, and felt a moral responsibility toward him, standing in front of me and confessing this grave matter.

Why me? Why did Tallan choose to confide in me, when I was a stranger to him? I didn't have an answer; fate has its wisdom.

I was weak when faced with others' needs for my help. I never hesitated to help strangers, so how could I stay silent when the person in need was close to me? How could I not extend my hand and support someone whom I had come to consider as a part of my family? How could I turn my back on him after realizing my attraction to Tallan and what that implied about me being as different as all of them?

If Miles were in a predicament, he wouldn't face it alone. If he were scared and didn't know how to act, I would stand by him and help him reach safety. I didn't hesitate to approach him. I hugged him strongly. I let him lean on my shoulder and cry out his fears until he calmed down and felt safe that I hadn't turned against him. I then helped him sit and assured him that we would find a solution for the two of them. There was no need to be afraid.

I wanted to ask him about her, his relationship, and his feelings toward her. I felt that day there was a large part of his life that I was unaware of. I wondered how he could be so talkative and open yet share so little about his attraction, love, and relationships.

I was curious about him, but it wasn't the right time, so I tried to change the conversation. I talked to him about different things and casually asked him about Tallan. I posed the question calmly, sipping my coffee as if it were one of those trivial matters that popped up from time to time.

"Do you know someone named Tallan?"

21

What Kind of Monsters Did This to You

"Tallan from the Skys family?

"Of course, I know him very well. Who doesn't know Tallan?" Miles added without waiting for my response.

My heart raced as he repeated the name I was so eager to hear. I listened to him speak of his acquaintance with Tallan. But my joy lasted only a moment, as he then shocked me by telling me that the love of my life had been admitted to the hospital two weeks ago after suffering an assault during the coronation festivities of the new king.

I gasped loudly, feeling dizzy and a warmth flooding my veins. "Who attacked him? How is he? Which hospital is he in? Can I visit him?" All those questions raced through my mind, as I stood frozen before Miles, unable to comprehend what he had just said. I didn't wait another moment. I forgot about Miles and the trouble he had gotten himself into. I jumped from where I stood, unsure of which direction to head in. I grabbed his arm, pulled him behind me, and asked him to accompany me immediately to the hospital where Tallan was being treated.

On the way, I didn't stop asking him what he knew of Tallan and the details of the incident.

He didn't know much. He told me he had only met Tallan a few times, having encountered him in that café through mutual friends. News of the attack on Tallan had spread among them, filling them with fear. They were all aggrieved by what had happened and felt unsafe now, in this city filled with hatred and intolerance.

When he had the chance to ask about my relationship with Tallan and the reason for my concern, I blushed, feeling like a teenager too embarrassed to admit my heart's desires. Although the situation wasn't ideal, I confessed to him about the romantic relationship between Tallan and me.

When we reached the hospital, I left him behind. I ran to the information desk and asked for the room number where Tallan was. I went to a flower kiosk and chose a bouquet of jasmines, the ones he loved. Holding them, my heart pounding hard, I went upstairs to the second floor, with Miles following me to Tallan's room. As I approached his room, I hesitated momentarily, fearing what I might see. But I pulled myself together, opened the door, and went in.

He smiled when he saw me, his beautiful face expressing surprise at my presence. He greeted me with a smile despite the evident pain on his face.

I approached him and reached for his hand, unable to believe what had happened to him. His right leg was elevated on a platform, wrapped by a white cast. Similarly, his left arm was in a cast from the elbow to the hand, with only his slender fingers visible. An IV was connected to his right arm, administering medication directly into his veins. His head was wrapped with white gauze, covering his wounds. His face and body were covered with bruises.

I nearly cried visiting him two weeks after the accident; it must have been even worse when he was first brought in. I took his head and gently kissed it. "What kind of monsters did this to you?" I felt an anger I hadn't experienced before. Breathing heavily, he revealed that his kidney had been bleeding when he arrived at the hospital, and they had to remove it in an emergency surgery.

"Did the police catch them?

"Did they bring them to justice?"

I pressed him for answers, but he remained silent, looking defeated, sorrowful, devoid of any hope or joy.

That completely crushed me.

He couldn't verbally share the details of what happened that night, but he wrote them down for me a few days later, after he had calmed down and felt comfortable and secure with my presence and support during this ordeal.

22

Tallan's Testimony

I heard the public call to head to the Grand River to attend the funeral of the queen and the inauguration of the new king. Like others in the city, I didn't dare disobey royal orders, especially when the announcement was urgent. And I knew it was dangerous to move among such large crowds in my natural state without a disguise that could either add to my height or make me seem shorter.

That day, I decided that joining the ceremony as a short might be the safest option. I was alone at home without any short companion. Going out as a tall alone among crowds, I would be prone to bullying and harassment, especially with the vertical line on my forehead indicating my bachelor's status. I could have cheated and drawn a fake horizontal line that complemented the vertical line to show that I was married. I would appear to be a married tall, not a single tall, which would help me obtain social protection in one way or another. But I hesitated to do so because the street was full of shortpolice, and the possibility of someone stopping me to verify my identity was high. Moreover, bad luck started before I left home as I couldn't find the ID that I use when I go out as a tall. Therefore,

I decided to go out as a short. That was the best solution given the current circumstances. Appearing as a married short would earn me greater respect in front of the crowd; no one would go so far as to ask me about my tall spouse or question my identity.

I stood in front of my mirror and imagined the crowd's reaction if I came out to them as a short with a vertical line drawn on my forehead. It would certainly be funny to some and provocative to others. I shook off the idea, picked up the eyeliner, and drew a horizontal line crossing the vertical line. I put on a thick wig to cover my bald head and a wide green dress with puffy pillows inside it to make me look fatter, and I went out.

I arrived at the city square and joined the crowd. I was pleased to meet a number of my friends of average height who had followed my example and disguised themselves in acceptable shapes. They all came with families who protected and helped to cover up for them, so I had to separate from them and finish the ceremony alone.

I headed toward the rows of shorts and chose a space in the last row. I did not feel comfortable, because an impolite group of single young shorts lined up next to me. I tried to avoid them at first and didn't react to the dirty jokes and rude comments they made. I did not comment on their throwing garbage in front of me on the ground without any respect for public space. I tried to move a few steps away from them when their jostling intensified, and their verbal exchanges turned into unpleasant physical clashes and collisions between hefty bodies. The size of their bodies made me feel intimidated. Despite the thickness of the pillows that I carried inside my dress, my size seemed small compared to theirs.

I made a mistake when the Royal Anthem began to play, and everyone stood in silence and reverence except for these teenagers, who continued to make jokes and laugh as if they were watching a comedy show. They had no respect for the moment, so I couldn't control my anger. I dared to look one teenager in the eye to make her feel ashamed and urge her to be silent. I was surprised when she looked back at me rudely. She shook her head, denouncing my interference in her affairs. She whispered something in her friend's ear and they both burst out in laughter as if they were deliberately provoking me. I gathered my courage, straightened my posture, looked at her directly, and said sharply in a loud voice, "Please, stay quiet. Show respect for the national anthem."

She responded quickly and dismissively, "Mind your own business."

I felt provoked by her answer and replied angrily, "You are in a public space, you should respect the situation and remain silent, just like everyone else, until the national anthem is over."

"Mind your own business and don't meddle in others' affairs," she snapped back at me.

The attendees noticed our heated argument and raised voices, urging us to calm down as if I were the one who started the disturbance. "Shush! Shush! Shush!"

The crowds tried to silence us, so I suppressed my anger and didn't respond. I turned my face away to continue watching the crowning ceremony and ignored her insult *while she spoke to her friend, commenting on what happened loud enough for me to hear, "Such an idiot!"*

Moments later, I requested to switch places and stood beside others on the opposite side, trying to distance myself from that aggressive girl and her annoying group.

After the ceremony ended, as I was about to leave the city square and move to the other side of the bridge to return home, I found her standing with her friends not far from me. I had forgotten the incident and didn't expect her to hold a grudge against me. She stood silently, staring.

As soon as she saw me, she left her friends and approached me aggressively, followed by one of them, who was even heavier and bulkier than her. She came close with visible hostility, put her face close to mine, and shouted, "How dare you speak to me like that?"

With her aggressive approach, I felt forced to step back, feeling fear facing her with all that obvious hostility. I'm not a fighter and didn't intend to get involved in a fight impulsively, especially against a group of teenagers younger by years.

Knowing the size of her body and of her friends meant I would be on the losing side in this brawl. I didn't know how to react. I said nothing when she again closed the distance that I had created by stepping back. She asked her question again with the same hostility, "Tell me, how dare you speak to me like that?"

She raised her large arms and opened her clenched fist, slapping me across the face. Following that, in a swift move I didn't expect, she pushed me hard backward.

Although the cushion I had around my chest absorbed most of the push, I felt my body lift into the air, traveling an arm's distance backward before collapsing to the ground. I was lucky; I didn't get hurt because the other cushions around my body protected me. But I was embarrassed, as this happened in front of a large group of people in the public square. They all stood astonished, silently watching the scene without intervening.

I almost jumped up angrily to confront her, to push her the way she pushed me to reclaim some of my dignity. But I feared the brawl would escalate and my true height would be revealed to everyone, so I hurried to gather my scattered cushions inside my clothes before anyone could notice. I was horrified when one slipped and fell to the floor in front of everyone, so I quickly retreated.

I didn't look at her because I didn't want to see her. I was afraid of provoking her anger if our eyes met. I walked in the opposite direction, silent, lowering my head in shame for what had happened, hoping she would leave me alone and not indulge in humiliating me. But behind me, I heard her cursing me and threatening me. Still, I ignored her and continued my way toward the bridge.

I stood in the queue. But bad luck was still haunting me. The shortpolice were overseeing the return of talls from the opposite side and merging them with their peers. The passage for shorts to cross to the other side was not open yet. I had to wait for an hour.

Unfortunately, what happened was just the beginning of my ordeal. After the opening of the bridge, I moved to the opposite side, heading toward my home. I heard a loud commotion coming from a group of young shorts not far behind me. When I dared to look back, I was horrified to recognize them. They were the same group that had bullied me just hours ago.

At first, I didn't realize they were following me, so I walked faster to avoid another confrontation. However, they, too, were fast. My heart raced as they shouted and called me a deviant. I realized that my secret had been exposed when I fell in the courtyard, and now they were chasing me with the intent to harm me. I had no choice but to run as fast as I could, trying to escape them. The sun was setting, and night enveloped the city. Without reasoning, I thought it might be best to go through the forest to disappear from their sight. I was sure they would parade me in public, and no one would intervene. Probably, the crowd would even cheer and join in the torment if they knew I was a medium.

What I did after was not wise! After running a short distance into the woods, I could hear their footsteps getting closer. I looked around for a dark corner to hide in and saw a tree with a split trunk. I quickly hid behind it, trying to catch my breath. I sat under it, holding my breath and trying to shrink myself as much as possible. Soon, I heard them just a few feet away.

"Where did he go?" they wondered aloud.

"He must be hiding around here somewhere. Keep looking."

It felt like a mission. A group of hungry hyenas searching for their prey. As they approached, I noticed flashes of light around me. One of them had pulled out a flashlight. Being discovered was now a matter of seconds.

I huddled closer, praying for salvation from this pre-dicament. I prepared to bolt and run if they discovered my hiding place. But it seemed that even the gods were against me that night, probably angered by my existence too.

Suddenly, the light was pointing directly at me, blinding me.

The same girl stood behind me, gloating proudly that she found me. "Here he is," she announced to her friends as I tried to escape.

This time, they were faster than me. They surrounded me from all directions and knocked me to the ground. They competed in slapping, kicking, and cursing me. With every slap and kick, their brutality flared. It seemed my weakness and vulnerability only fueled them, pushing them to act like wild animals.

I begged them to stop, but they didn't listen. One of them grabbed my head and covered my mouth with his hand so I couldn't utter a word. The others' hands ripped my clothes into shreds, using them to gag me and tie my hands behind my back.

After ensuring I was gagged, they continued to strip me. They left me naked at their mercy and threw me to the ground. The girl approached me and asked her friend to lift me off the ground to face her. She slapped me and said, "This is to teach you not to disobey your masters."

She exposed her large breast, removed the gag from my mouth, and forcefully pushed it in while gripping my head tightly, ordering me to suck it as if I were a sex slave in her palace. At the same time, her friend lifted his robe, revealing his thick penis. He grabbed my rear and forcefully entered me. He firmly gripped me from behind and forced me to sit with his back to the tree. I couldn't escape his grip. The girl continued her assault, showing off her vagina, making sure my penis was hard enough before she sat on me with her large thighs apart, letting her heavy body weigh on mine, leaving me breathless.

They crushed me from both sides as if I were a piece of meat. The rest of the gang then took turns assaulting me, each in turn, until I lost consciousness.

I only regained awareness in the hospital as nurses prepared me for the operating room.

23

How Can I Erase That
from My Memory

Tallan finally finished documenting the assault after I had repeatedly pleaded that it must be written down even if he didn't want to report it to the police. Writing about the incident would help him, as he was barely eating his food and refused to tell me any details about what happened. It was as if he felt ashamed and blamed himself for it.

I hadn't left his side since I first came to visit him. And I insisted on taking him home after his release from the hospital so I could care for him. Luckily, the personal ID he had on him confirmed that he was a short, so there was no official obstacle preventing me from taking him to my house. Days later, when I felt that his mood had improved, I seized the opportunity, handed him a piece of paper and a pen, and asked him to write down what had happened.

I returned after an hour, only to be surprised that he had detailed the incident meticulously, with all its harshness and pain. I took it to my room and read it. I wish I hadn't. I almost tore it up as what was in it felt more than

I could bear. I wanted to crush it under my feet, burn it, erase it from existence. I cursed my curiosity for wanting to know what had happened to him. I cursed the world that allowed such a crime to take place.

How can I erase it from my memory?

How can I erase its marks from his body?

How can I bring life back to his soul after they had snuffed out any glimmer of hope from him?

My teardrops fell on the handwritten account of his destruction. I wiped at them, smudging the ink. The words would not disappear. I stored it in a special file in my safe. I rephrased it later to fit the language in which I am writing this story.

I held it as if holding onto a burning fire.

And I swore to the Gods of the Sun and the Great River that I would bring him justice and restore his status, making him a king with his head held high.

24

Rocky Was the Last
Thing We Needed

It was painful watching Tallan suffer, but his presence in my home filled a void in my heart, as if him being near me added warmth to my life. With Miles's presence, full of good humor and lively chatter, I felt the growth of a family bond that united the three of us; a sense I missed since I left my parents' house, moved to this bleak city, and decided to live here alone.

Rocky was really the last thing we needed. I knew her position about Tallan. I understood her beliefs and knew her way of thinking. I knew she wouldn't hesitate to carry out her threat against me. She wouldn't let me host him in my house. The news of her new pregnancy gave me the perfect excuse to grant her a paid, open-ended leave. I called her the night I brought Tallan with me from the hospital and told her I had contracted measles. I warned her about approaching the area so she wouldn't catch the infection and harm the baby. I warned her repeatedly about its rapid spread so she wouldn't stubbornly come to visit. I reminded her of her fatigue during the first months of her first pregnancy, then assured her about the presence of Miles to cover for her during her absence.

"Family first," I reminded her, for I knew her values very well.

"Family first," she echoed my words in agreement.

I knew she hated sitting at home without work, for we, shorts, feel suffocated between the walls of enclosed spaces. Being with Pole and Ray all the time would drive her mad. And Ray's jealousy was already at its peak after Rocky's second pregnancy from Pole. She was surely going to cause more problems. But I wouldn't worry about Rocky or think about her family. I would let her deal with her matters while I dealt with mine, as I had no time to think of the mess Miles got himself into, with Tallan occupying my every thought.

Miles was blinded by love, as if he had forgotten the severity of what happened or couldn't fathom the gravity of the issue at hand. Soon, Willow's pregnancy would start showing. We couldn't predict how her family would deal with this disaster. They might kill her, or force her to reveal the father's identity and then kill them both, or make her abort the child to hide the shame.

He had brought her to my house a few days ago to visit Tallan with a group of common friends. After that, she began coming every day, helping Miles with his duties and spending long hours with us. I had never seen a romantic relationship between two people of the same height. It felt strange to me, even though they were cautious in expressing their feelings in front of me. I was capturing love in their glances at each other, and found it endearing. Their affection became more evident after they got comfortable and stopped being shy. Their loving glances eventually translated into physical closeness, and they never parted. It was as if a strong magnet drew them together, as if there was immense attraction that they couldn't resist.

I understood it because I, too, felt that force was drawing me to Tallan.

I looked at them as they melted in each other's arms, planting sweet kisses on each other's lips; Miles kisses Willow's forehead, Willow holds his hand and kisses it. Miles does the same and holds her hand and kisses it, Willow gets closer to him and kisses his neck. Miles moves his face and kisses her cheek, Willow looks into his eyes and moves her lips closer to his and kisses him, once, twice, and more.

Every time that happens, I quietly withdraw into the kitchen or the bathroom or Tallan's room to see if he needs anything, to draw a sketch, or to complete the work on a new dress.

That day, while I was in the room with Tallan, I had an idea that I thought might be the solution to their problem. I was preparing the tools to shave his head; his hair had grown long and needed shaving. I usually don't find beauty in the hair of talls but it was strangely attractive on Tallan's head. I loved feeling the hair growing on his head. I loved it even more when it became longer, softer, and thicker. He was used to shaving regularly and was not comfortable with hair on his head. His appearance was indeed more beautiful without it because he looked more like a tall than a short, which I preferred. And since I didn't dare bring a groomer to my house, as they might have suspicions about Tallan and my relationship with him, I decided to take on this task myself.

I helped him sit on the wheelchair that I provided for him and pushed him toward the bathroom, where he could watch himself in the mirror as I shaved him. I wrapped a towel around his neck and applied shaving cream. I lifted the razor and gently passed it over his scalp. I was hesitant to propose my idea to him and I didn't know how he would react to it. He knew about Miles's relationship with Willow, but he didn't know yet that she was pregnant.

I told him straight after rinsing his head when I finished shaving. "Willow is pregnant." I awaited his reaction after he wiped his head and face. He opened his eyes in shock. "What?!"

"Yes, I understand the seriousness of the matter. I don't know how we can help," I confirmed what I said without rushing to propose my solution.

"How far is she?"

"She's still in the first trimester."

"If she's still in the early stages, we might be able to fix things."

I understood what he was suggesting. I replied that I had proposed the idea to Miles, and he confirmed his refusal. Willow wanted to keep the baby.

"This is dangerous for her and Miles's life. We need to convince her to change her mind." He seemed afraid, convinced that persuading her to give up the child was the only solution.

I paused momentarily as I pulled his wheelchair back to his room. "Tallan, in your official ID, you are registered as short, right?"

He seemed surprised by my question and replied irritably as if he didn't like admitting that. "Yes."

I was expecting that answer even though I didn't like hearing it. Maybe I couldn't accept the truth because I didn't want to accept that I was a deviant attracted to another short. I realized the truth of what was written on his ID the day I finished his official papers in the hospital. I tried to forget about it, but on that day, I saw how an unpleasant truth could become useful. Being registered as a short meant I couldn't marry him. However, that wouldn't pose an obstacle if he agreed to my suggestion and married Willow.

"I have a solution to the problem without having to get rid of the child," I said in a tone devoid of emotion.

"What is it?" he asked curiously.

"Marry her."

"Me?" He was taken aback by my suggestion. "Why me?"

"I initially considered Rocky but Rocky is a female, and Willow can't get pregnant by her. And I don't know any other short who is a male that I can trust with this issue," I explained to him. "You know how much I love you. It is hard for me as much as it is hard for you.

"It will be a marriage in name only, and I will accompany you through all stages until we overcome this tough period," I assured him.

I looked into his eyes with hope and asked, "What do you think?"

25

We Had to Prepare Tallan for the Wedding

We gathered around the breakfast table on a beautiful sunny morning. In addition to Miles and Willow, the short who thinks of herself as a tall joined us; the same short whom I found peculiar in her appearance and movements in that strange hidden café, the place where I met Willow for the first time. To my dismay, Celestia turned out to be Tallan's closest friend. I had to accept her for his sake, so I invited her for a meal to make him happy and to get to know her better.

Speaking to her that day, I was cautious. I was careful with every word before saying it, ensuring that I addressed her using talls' pronouns the way she likes to present herself, to avoid disrespecting her unintentionally. It would be inappropriate to address her using shorts' pronouns, disregarding her choice of appearance, behavior, and expression, just because her bones were short. Offending her this way would upset Tallan, which I could never bear. I wanted him free of worries and sadness. He deserved happiness, especially after the horrendous incident he went through.

Despite the cruelty of the assault, what happened did not strip him of his humanity. He was noble and didn't disappoint me when I suggested marrying Willow. His gallant reaction made me admire him even more: His eyes widened in surprise and his mouth opened in amazement. His reaction surprised me as he praised my suggestion, exclaiming, "What a smart idea!"

He said it with a passion missing from his face recently, which made me feel a burning urge to kiss him. I felt that he understood me and thought like me. He knew that what united us was more genuine than official papers; he believed that our love was more potent than the confines society has created and that our love could birth new meanings every day. Despite everything and everyone, we became a family.

The four of us were in the same boat. We had to face reality and stand united.

The more I got to know Tallan, the more evident it became that his chivalry wasn't out of character. He consistently built a network of relationships with those like him for mutual support. Despite the hardships he had faced in his life, he refused to play the victim. He dealt with his reality with strength and intelligence, planning for a better life for himself and those around him.

However, things were different with Miles, who completely rejected the idea when I asked him to join us in Tallan's room and informed him about the plan. He was taken aback and resisted. He perceived the idea with his immature rebellious spirit and opposed it. He stood defiantly, condemning my words, claiming it was a submission to the status quo and an acceptance of reality that would further entrench injustice.

"Do you want me to live a lie? To be a hypocrite and abandon my principles?" He raised his hand, shouting.

His reaction took us aback. We had to step in to restrain his impulsiveness when he went overboard in his speech declaring, "We will not succumb to them. We will not surrender to their values, nor will we accept their morals. By dawn, we will leave this awful place and abandon it to them."

Was escaping into the unknown the solution? Would the solution be to move to another country and live among other people who harbor similar thoughts and practice the same hatred for those who are different?

He might have been right that day but we wouldn't allow him to leave. We talked until we managed to convince him that this was the only solution possible. It wasn't the ideal solution, but it was the only one for his safety, for the safety of his beloved, and for the safety of their unborn child.

"You will be strangers wherever you go, both of you and your child. You are pushing yourself and your family into the unknown with your recklessness and inability to cope with reality," I accused him in a desperate attempt to bring him back to his senses.

He stayed lost in thought for a while, then reluctantly agreed to our plan. Despite this tentative acceptance, we worried that he might change his mind and disappear with her. Fortunately, Willow was more rational than he was. She didn't resist when we met with her and proposed the idea. She was deeply affected; tears filled her eyes. She held Miles's hand as if she couldn't believe there was a solution to their predicament. "You don't have to do this for us," she said, trying to gauge our determination. "But that means you won't be able to formally bond?" She was puzzled about how to deal with the awkward situation. How could she refuse when we offered her something that would shape our future and theirs?

"We don't care about formal papers," Tallan replied.

I added from my side, "We are like you; we cannot formally register our love because Tallan is registered as a short in civil records."

"You can request a modification," she directed her words to Tallan, suggesting a solution for us. "You are a medium, and the law allows it for mediums."

Tallan wasn't ready to get involved in legal risks that might require months or even years to convince the world to change his height on paper for a different identity that might deprive him of more rights than it gives. He wasn't concerned about being tall or short in people's eyes as much as being able to help himself and his loved ones.

We calmed her down and explained that we under-stood the consequences of our decision and were prepared for whatever comes. "The space in my house is sufficient for all of us. We will divide it visually in front of people; one house for you and Tallan and the other for me so that I can be close to you both," I laid out a plan before her.

"And Miles?" she asked.

"Both houses are his. Formally, in people's eyes, he will stay here at his workplace as usual, but in reality, he will be with you, as your partner and the father of your child," I answered with an encouraging smile.

She was convinced and welcomed the idea. She approached me, hugged me, and then hugged Tallan. Her gesture moved me, so I opened my arms to hug them both. I looked at Miles and extended my arms, inviting him to join us.

That day, the four of us (five if you count the baby in her womb) embraced. I wished that embrace to be a lasting image for our future. However, the next day we started preparing Tallan to look like a real short, as Willow's family would not hesitate to reject him in his current form, in a confusing state between talls and shorts.

We raced against time and worked on fattening him up faster than the rate at which the fetus was growing in Willow's belly. We needed him to get round and chubby and swollen; we needed his hair to grow and flow over his head like any other healthy strong short.

Although the matter was strange to both of us, I did not know if my feelings would change with his change in appearance. He was not accustomed to that form, he was not ready to play that role, and he felt annoyed with the thick hair growing over his head. However, I enjoyed feeding him and filling his mouth with food. I prepared ten eggs every morning with a large plate of cheese and another of sausages for him. I broke an entire loaf of bread, thickly spread with layers of homemade ghee specifically made for fattening adolescent shorts. I placed bite after bite in his mouth and urged him to swallow as my grandmother did with me during my teenage years.

He would choke when I placed more food than he could handle in his mouth. That's when I would see his eyes bulge, and I would hurry to pat his back until he spit out what had gotten stuck in his throat. Then, I would give him a bigger sip of water and apologize, laughing at what had happened. I didn't learn, though; I repeated the same thing as if I had inherited this from my grandmother or saw it as an opportunity to do to him what was done to me.

One day, after I had stuffed him with more than he could chew, he ran to the bathroom and vomited everything he had eaten. He came back shivering.

"Enough! I don't want to be a short anymore!"

I joked to lighten the mood, "We, shorts, have many privileges but they come at a price."

He was willing to pay the price and was determined not to back down from his decision no matter what I did to him. He had already gained ten kilograms, when Celestia, who was visiting, got shocked. "Oh my God! What have you done to him?"

His cheeks had begun to round, his belly swelled, his thighs thickened, and his hair had become half a finger long, covering his head like a hedgehog's short, spiky coat. When Celestia sat down at the breakfast table and saw the dishes stacked around him and watched me feed him, she put her hand over her mouth and gasped, protesting, "No, I can't see this!

"How do you bear what's being done to you?"

We laughed at her reaction because seeing the process seemed more painful to her than it was for him.

Tallan, chewing on a whole egg I stealthily slipped into his mouth, remarked, "Seeing you like this reminds me of our teenage days when you used to come to me running away from your father."

"Oh, no! Don't you remind me!" she shook her head, her expression turning to anger. "He wanted to fatten me up by any means, but I didn't want to gain weight. We argued daily. He was stubborn and I was more stubborn than him."

She continued, grabbing our attention with her story, "He would get my brothers to hold me down so I couldn't move while he stuffed food into my mouth. When I spat it out, knowing his intentions, he would slap me across the face, pull my hair hard and try to open my mouth again to force-feed me. I hated my appearance, hair, and life during that period. I insisted I was tall, determined to stand out as tall despite their attempts to convince me otherwise. My biggest fear back then, and still to a large extent today, was that I'd die, and my ashes would be thrown into the Big River instead of in the desert, just as the ashes of shorts were scattered upon their death. I used to head to the desert every week and beg the gods to guide me. Several times, I exposed myself to the scorching Sun for hours, ready to die and give up my soul, ensuring I would join the souls of the talls. I never had enough strength to stay under it longer than my energy allowed. When I started hallucinating, I cooled down by dipping my head into a bucket of water and prayed that the gods would forgive me. Over time, my suicidal tendencies weakened and my faith in the gods became weaker."

She continued recalling her story, "I remember one time I went into my bathroom and took the scissors. I wanted to cut my vein to end my life, but I couldn't. I was scared. I didn't even pass the scissors on my wrist. Instead, I started cutting my hair. Strand by strand until I was completely bald."

She smiled as if she was replaying the scene. "I felt a relief that day, watching it fall over my face and shoulders and covering the bathroom floor."

The scene seemed terrifying and sad. Yet, she added with pride and a smile, "That was the first time I announced my freedom. It was also the last time I saw my father."

Surprised by her bravery, after asking Miles to bring more bread from the kitchen, I inquired, "What do you mean it was the last time you saw your father?"

"He lost his mind when he saw me without hair. He grabbed my arm forcefully, dragged me, and threw me out of the house, threatening that I should never return," she replied without showing any emotions, as if the story weren't about her.

"And I never returned."

"What did you do? How did you survive at such a young age?" Miles asked, curious about the story after returning from the kitchen.

"She wandered the streets for a week before I found her in a pitiful condition. I took her by the hand and persuaded her to come with me to my mother, and I did my best to convince mom to host her until we found a solution for her issue," Tallan replied.

I smiled, listening to how Tallan had saved her in the same way he was helping Miles and Willow today.

"How beautiful your mother was, Tallan! I miss her so much!" Celestia said, recalling the kindness his mother showed her. "She was still sad about the loss of your father and hadn't yet recovered from the shock of your growth stabilizing at an average height."

He nodded in agreement as she continued, "I will never forget the look on her face when you brought me to your house. She didn't know how to handle it, and she couldn't bear another calamity added to her burden. Despite my short hair and her discomfort with our friendship, her humanity was greater than leaving me out on the streets without shelter. She welcomed me into her home until I contacted my aunt and ensured I would be safe with her."

"I think she was worried about me. Worried about my future and my ability to make friends, being a medium. She felt Celestia resembled me in a way or another, so accepted her the way she accepted me," Tallan explained.

How beautiful was the love Tallan's mother had for him! How touching was what she was willing to do for him! How strange was it that I felt the same way about him since the moment I saw him?

Love, concern, and a desire to protect and make him happy.

I was enjoying that conversation. I was happy with this beautiful family gathering when I heard a persistent and sharp knock on the door as if something urgent was happening.

I left them and rushed to open the door, only to be surprised by Rocky's presence.

26

She Believes Violence Disciplines Talls

I hurried when I saw Rocky approaching the entrance. I didn't expect her to ignore my warning about visiting me during this period after I informed her of my measles infection. Her presence concerned me. I feared her reaction upon seeing the gathering in my house. I remembered what she said about Tallan after his first visit, which made me fear her rage when her eyes fell on Celestia and noticed her appearance, her clothes, and the way she carried herself.

Her knocks on the door were quick and consecutive, as if she came due to some urgent matter that couldn't wait. I read that in her face when I opened the door for her, but stood in the opening, blocking the entrance with my bulky body, wondering about the reason for her sudden arrival.

I was not able to stop her in her agitated, angry state. "That crazy bitch left the house."

"What? Who are you talking about?" I asked her as I made way for her to enter.

She rushed in like a missile. Or, to describe her more accurately, considering her size and her angry face, she stormed in like a ticking bomb launched by a long-range cannon. In either case, be it a bomb or a missile, I couldn't steer her away from the guest room. I realized this after she reached the room and stood before everyone inside. Despite her rush and her surprise at their presence, she composed herself and greeted them.

"Hello!"

They all replied with faces full of astonishment, "Hello you!"

Only Miles knew her and was equally concerned about her sudden arrival.

She stood silent for a moment and looked at me, waiting for me to introduce her to them. I hesitated for a moment, trying to contain the situation. Fortunately, her haste didn't allow her to notice anything odd; she didn't recognize Tallan after his weight gain and the soft hair that grew to cover up his previously bald head, she didn't notice the awkwardness in how Celestia presented herself because she was seated, and she didn't pick up on the love relationship between Miles and Willow in that brief time.

Likewise, she didn't think to check my face for the measles spots I had warned her about.

"Rocky, my assistant," I introduced her to them and excused myself. I ushered her toward the fabric room and closed the door behind us, wondering what caused her anger. I was sure the issue was about Ray, and my assumption was correct.

"Ray left the house."

I wasn't surprised because it wasn't the first time Ray had left her house to return to her family. Their problems never ended and Rocky never hesitated to use violence in an attempt to discipline her. Lately, her aggression toward Ray concerned me as it grew more severe and harmful. I had also expected the rise in tension between them due to Rocky's pregnancy and her need to stay for an extended amount of time at home with Ray and Pole, but I didn't anticipate it would reach this point!

"What happened?"

"I unintentionally broke her arm. Her family is very upset this time and refuse to send her back home. They demand I divorce her."

"WHAT DID YOU DO?!" I screamed at her. I didn't want to believe what I heard! "How in the hell did you 'unintentionally' break her arm?"

It was unusual for me to talk to Rocky in that tone, as she was my best friend, and I loved her dearly. At the same time, I knew that Ray's attitude provoked me. I believed she was a dishonest person and was cunning to no limits; nevertheless, I disliked the way Rocky treated her spouses, and I disapproved of her use of violence to solve her family issues.

Every time we argued about this matter, it was pointless. I always backed down after she ended the argument by claiming that her relationship with Ray was a family matter I shouldn't interfere with. She was as stubborn as a rock. She believed it was permissible to hit talls for disciplinary purposes, ignoring the fact that the world had changed and such a practice was no longer accepted as it was in previous generations.

That day, I couldn't remain silent about what she had done. She hadn't just hit her spouse, she had broken her arm too. On top of that, she shamelessly asked me to mediate for her with Ray's family, even though I had done so many times before! I vouched for her and promised them that she would control her reactions and never lay a hand on her spouse again.

"For the love of Gods, I didn't mean to break it," she swore.

She continued her story, explaining how Ray had provoked her since early that morning. She hadn't slept much that night because the pregnancy was exhausting her, and she woke up to the sound of the baby crying and to the sound of Ray and Pole arguing about a trivial household matter and how they should distribute tasks between them. Despite feeling nauseous and dizzy, her intense anger took over. She grabbed her bamboo stick from her closet, rushed toward them without thinking, and violently hit both of them with the stick, punishing them for their "misbehavior" as she put it. Pole, as usual, was conciliatory. He apologized to her and didn't run away from her stick. He endured the pain even though he wasn't the one who caused the problem. However, Ray ran upstairs to hide in her room, betting on her agility and speed, assuming that, due to Rocky's weight and pregnancy, she wouldn't be able to catch up before Ray could close and lock the door. But Rocky was faster than Ray expected. She caught her on the stairs and cornered her between the two floors. She raised her stick to continue disciplining her. To Rocky's surprise, Ray tried to grab the stick, attempting to snatch it from Rocky's hands as she couldn't bear the pain of being beaten.

She resisted with all her might. Thinking she might succeed, given the height advantage she had, she tried to pull the stick upward. When Rocky realized what Ray was attempting to do, she leveraged her physical strength and body size. She pulled the stick toward herself violently, pushing Ray, who was caught off guard.

Ray felt herself flying, curling up, and rolling down the stairs.

"I didn't realize at the time that she had fallen on her arm and broken it," Rocky claimed. "I thought she was just pretending, as usual, and that she was exaggerating to make me stop hitting her."

Ray didn't stop crying. After an hour, her forearm swelled, and her arm became alarmingly inflamed, which led Rocky to take her to the hospital. There, they told the doctor about the fall but did not mention how it had occurred, fearing Rocky would be prosecuted. Although Rocky apologized to her and tried to reconcile that night, Ray disappeared the next morning. She ran away to her family's house and decided not to return. Now, Rocky was here, asking me to help her bring her back.

After telling me the full story, she looked at me as if she was searching for something, "Are you sure it's measles?"

I had anticipated this question but didn't prepare an answer. I lied to her, claiming it was just an allergic reaction and that I had mistaken it for measles.

She didn't challenge my claim.

27

I Was Saddened by the Realization That We Were Distorting Ourselves to Please Others

I excused myself from my guests and went out with Rocky. We headed toward her in-laws' house and met with the shorts of Ray's family. We sat with them around a cup of coffee and accomplished the task. We apologized to them and reconciled with Ray after Rocky promised, in writing this time and with me as a witness, not to resort to violence to discipline her spouses from now on.

On my way back, I felt disgusted with what happened. My conscience was pricking me. How could I allow myself to be a tool of oppression after I got close to Tallan, Miles, Willow, and Celestia, and knew the suffering they faced because of height-based discrimination? After I had formed a special family with them, a family that has its own rules and structures away from those outdated customs and traditions? I was annoyed by Rocky's rigid thinking and was provoked by her way of living and how she treated her spouses and those around her. I reproached myself for my weakness, for my inability to refuse her. I resented being dragged into situations governed by false traditions that no longer represented me.

I felt I embodied the true meaning of hypocrisy as I sat among them in the shorts' room, spreading my buttocks on the couch and stretching my chubby legs on the ornate carpet, holding the coffee cup on my belly as if I were one of them, with their values, morals, and customs. I raised the tone of my voice and said with feigned seriousness what is often mentioned in such situations, "We, shorts, are emotional about matters concerning our families and their welfare. We all know that such problems occur in most homes. What happened was no more than an accident that Rocky did not intend. She did not mean to hurt Ray. She only wanted to discipline her for the sake of the family." I shamelessly used the excuse of shorts' inability to control their emotions.

I clarified to them that the motive behind Rocky's outburst was her love for her family. Being the short in this relationship, she had every right to do what she saw fit. I felt nauseous while imagining Tallan sitting among them, looking at me with disgust, not believing that the short sitting there was the same one he loved and trusted. In my heart, I knew he had every right to scorn what I had done after all he had been through, from being raped to agreeing to marry Willow while he had not recovered yet, to enduring his face growing round and his limbs becoming chubby just like mine and Rocky's. He agreed to change his appearance and identity to please me, and I was failing him at the first opportunity!

I was saddened by the realization that we were distorting ourselves to please others, a reality that struck me as I stood there saying goodbye to Rocky before heading back to my family. I found myself wondering, why am I afraid to confess to her the truth of my love for Tallan when she is not ashamed about beating up her spouses? Why do we overlook the prevailing wrong and ignore what our truth manifests? Why do we neglect what our desires and needs clearly state?

Was Miles right in his inclination to revolt? Have we been wrong to succumb to the status quo, hiding under its fake sense of a stable and peaceful life, instead of confronting it and trying to change it?

I felt a strong urge to revolt as I rushed home toward Tallan to tell him of my shame for what I had done. I wanted to hug him and apologize. To promise him that I would not repeat what I had done and that I was not ashamed of my love for him. I would face Rocky if necessary and challenge the world for him.

Indeed, he could not believe his ears when I told him what had happened with Rocky and why I had left suddenly with her that morning. Although I expected his negative reaction, I did not expect it to be that harsh. His face changed to show the disgust I feared, and I saw the pain in his eyes, pain that I knew I had caused as if I had pressed on his wounds. I realized my fault and did not know how to act. I remained silent and did not defend myself when he shouted at me angrily and asked me in disbelief, "How could you do that? Who are you? I don't know you!"

"Sorry," I coughed hard and apologized. I tried to approach him, but he raised his hand in my face to stop me. "Rocky is my lifelong friend, and I cannot deny her in her time of need," I tried to justify my weakness. He was unwilling to hear me. He was not able to accept my justifications.

"And what about Ray?"

"She will be fine," I answered while trying to stop myself from accusing her of being the reason for everything that happened.

"And how do you know she will be fine?" he interrogated me, putting himself in her place.

"I know Rocky. She is kind-hearted and will not hurt her."

"And how do you guarantee she won't hurt her? This is not the first time she has resorted to violence against her spouses. Do you know how many talls have lost their lives at the hands of their short spouses in the past year?" He raised his voice, screaming.

I was silent, not knowing how to answer him because he was right. I didn't want to believe that Rocky was capable of harming her spouse that way. I didn't want to admit it despite the statistics, indicators, and data.

"Rocky is different," I told myself. It won't happen as he predicts.

"Or didn't that matter to you?" He was attacking me in a way I had never seen before.

"Of course not, because you are a short who takes pride in playing the role of the master. You, shorts, gather and decide what should and should not be done. What is appropriate and what is not? Are you happy that your friend's spouse returned to her? How is Rocky different from that short who assaulted me? Would you have stood by and watched her assault me because she is short like you? Or would you have joined them and participated in the assault?" He was agitated with an anger I had not seen in him before. I did not know how to handle the situation. I could not believe he was comparing me to that short and her friends who assaulted him. I was saddened that he allowed himself to think that I was capable of hurting him that way.

I didn't answer or respond to him, for I loved him. I knew he was venting out his pain and suffering. I tried to calm him down that night and begged him not to leave the house while he was in that state.

I withdrew to my room, fearing I would wake up to-morrow and find him gone.

28

I Became Obsessed
with One Idea

A strange idea came to me and took over my mind. I was anxious all night and couldn't sleep. A cough accompanied me, along with the fear of losing Tallan. In the morning, I got up and headed to his room to ensure he hadn't left. When I didn't find him in his room, I searched for him in the bathroom, the kitchen, and the living room. After nearly giving up hope of finding him, sadness overcame me, and I felt like crying.

I spotted him in the garden, reading a book.

For a moment, I wondered who this short sitting in my garden was, as I wasn't yet accustomed to his new appearance with the green robe, thick hair, and bulky body, and he wasn't usually comfortable sitting outside due to the scrutiny and comments of others.

I approached him and greeted him with a "good morning." I looked into his eyes to see if he was still upset with me after last night's argument.

"Good morning," he replied calmly, which comforted me.

As usual, he quietly asked, "How was your night? Did you sleep well?"

Although I hadn't slept that night, I responded with "yes" and returned the question.

"Regarding last night, I apologize for my aggressive reaction and the harsh words I said about you." His words moved me.

I also apologized, acknowledging my mistake and promised to take a firmer stance with Rocky. I would make it clear to her that under no circumstances would I tolerate her assaulting her spouses.

After exchanging apologies and clearing the air, I put my hand in his, indicating we had moved past our first argument. I drew closer to him, hugging and kissing his forehead, feeling grateful for his presence in my life.

I noticed he was reading the book *Shorts Are from Jupiter and Talls Are from Neptune*, which I had borrowed from Rocky, so I took the opportunity to change the mood and asked, "What do you think of the book?" knowing that the ideas in the book might provoke him.

"Where did you get it?"

I hesitated to respond as I didn't want to mention Rocky. I thought my acknowledgment of getting the book from her would upset him and reinforce his negative perception of her. Still, I replied after seeing the look in his eyes, which seemed to indicate he knew the answer, "From Rocky." I rushed to clarify that the book belonged to her spouse, Pole, as she doesn't read.

"Have you read it?"

"I've read some chapters but haven't finished it yet," I said.

"I liked the author's smooth style, his sense of humor, and how he backs up his claims with research findings. However, I wasn't convinced by a significant part of it. I felt he exaggerated in interpreting the data and his logic in connecting data to prove his point of view was weak." I added.

"I agree with you to a certain extent. There is a plethora of evidence that indicates differences between shorts and talls to such an extent that it led me to believe we might indeed be two separate species, as if we came from two different planets. However, I believe that all the differences listed by the author, except for actual height, aren't strictly biological but are results of social factors that have been exaggerated and culturally entrenched over a long period."

"Even biological height can't be considered a strict differentiating factor, as it varies between human beings and can't be clearcut on this matter," I added to his words, knowing that we had discussed this before and were in agreement.

I admit that my perception of social types had changed significantly since getting to know Tallan and Miles, discovering Miles's same-height attraction, and learning his views on various traits associated with tallness and shortness, and the social roles each entails. I had been thinking recently more deeply about this topic every time I found a moment for personal reflection. A few days ago, while I was sitting in the sewing room, a strange thought took over my mind. I was alone, listening to calm music, working on a new dress for Tallan suitable for his wedding night with Willow. I had to go back to the drawing board and start anew and design a dress suitable for shorts after he decided to take on this mission and abandon his dream of impressing everyone with his height and elegance on that family wedding night.

That day, I had placed the sewing needle on the pattern paper on top of the round table. Next to it, I placed the thimble. I set them a finger's distance apart and contemplated the difference in the length and the slender shape of the needle and the width of the thimble.

After a few seconds, I grabbed the sewing chalk I used to mark lines on the fabric and placed it halfway between the needle and the thimble. It wasn't as long or slender as the needle, and it wasn't as short or round as the thimble. I found it like Tallan. And, in my mind I connected its vital role in the sewing work to Tallan's role, with his average height, in a society that rejects him.

I took a pencil and wrote his name on the surface of the chalk. I picked it up, kissed it, and put it back in its place.

I began to hum the lyrics of the song I was listening to:

> *O Short-hearted one, O you tall in passion*
> *O icy mountain in a warm gulf*
> *Moved*
> *Back   and forth*
> *by the wind*
> *From here   to there*
> *Without affecting*
> *its mighty weight*

I paused at the song's lyrics, which seemed to reproach a tall lover, juxtaposing the rigid hearts of shorts with the frivolity of talls in love. I contemplated our distribution of traits between shorts and talls, and how forgiving we are, both in songs and to some extent in society, in combining a trait associated with shorts and a trait associated with talls in one person, regardless of whether the person is actually short or tall!

I wondered why we use height as a foundational trait to define ourselves, build our societal identity, and classify individuals in our human societies. I understood the historical explanation for widespread famines during the evolution of societies and the resulting distinction between shorts and talls. I appreciated the religious explanation that creation was made this way due to the collective desire of the deities of the Sun and Great River to reflect their characteristics on us. But what if reality wasn't like that?

What if our societies evolved to classify humanity based on a different biological trait other than height? How would they look? I started thinking.

At first, I considered color as the primary distinguishing factor. But, after a brief reflection, I realized that, although we classify people to some extent based on their skin color, this classification isn't the primary one in our societies. This might be because the gradient of skin color doesn't differ significantly in certain regions or among specific groups, as it's directly related to the surrounding environment and family genetics. Therefore, it might only be suitable for distinguishing between human groups, rather than individuals. Perhaps because human societies with similar skin colors were isolated from those different from them in ancient times, skin color wasn't given much weight as a foundational and essential human classification. Nevertheless, even today, we prefer that mating occurs between individuals of similar skin color rather than different ones. In this way, we reinforce skin color as a collective trait rather than an individual one.

Moreover, our collective consciousness mistakenly puts height in two categories rather than admitting it comes in a spectrum, which made me realize that skin color might not suit what I was contemplating, so I looked for another characteristic.

What if that characteristic were biological sex?

I understood that sexual organs were present among humans in a wide gradient and variety, just like skin color. However, biological sex was an individual characteristic closer to height in this context, and there was a clear distinction in this attribute among individuals across all races and human groups. This distinction might not have been as evident as the differences seen in height, but it became apparent when bodies were exposed. We could suggest two types of humans if cumulative social and cultural factors amplified this distinction over time.

We tended to describe human beings based on the size and protrusion of their sexual organs. Those whose sexual organs protruded in the chest area were described as females, and those in the pelvic area were described as males. Those with smaller organs that didn't prominently protrude in either region were described as intersex.

That day, I felt that the idea was viable for what I was searching for, so I let my imagination run wild to sketch a parallel world similar to ours, where humans are divided based on another biological trait, where two types of humans are created based on it. In my imagination, I began sketching out this world to be more empathetic toward Tallan.

Then, as I paused and listened to him speak about height, social types, and the public's ignorance of what that meant, I felt my heart dance in his presence, and my soul found solace in hearing his voice. An image of that parallel world appeared before me.

Knowing him to be a male, with his sexual organ protruding in the pelvic region, I decided to give preference to males in that world just as we prefer shorts in our world.

"Tallan, what if height wasn't the primary characteristic for dividing humans in our society?" I surprised him with my question.

"What? What do you mean?" He didn't grasp what I was hinting at.

"What if we divided humans based on their biological sex instead of their height?" I tried to simplify the idea for him.

He seemed puzzled. "Why would we classify humans in the first place? Isn't it better for us to combat division, classification, and discrimination among humans in all its forms and manifestations?"

I paused.

He was right.

Classifying humans based on a single attribute isn't right. But I felt I still wanted to embark on this thought experiment anyway. "I agree with you. It's best to fight all forms of discrimination among humans, but understanding social types is complex and intricate. Imagining its evolution differently might help us comprehend it more clearly. By seeing it from a different perspective and understanding its various dimensions, we might dismantle the social aura surrounding it and erase the illusory lines that support it," I explained.

After a moment of silence, in which he pondered what I had said, he replied, "Fine, let it be as you wish. But why did you choose sex as your base trait? Our biological sexual differences are minuscule and not that apparent."

"I disagree with you. Our biological sexual differences are not minuscule. It can certainly be exaggerated by tying it to other traits and linking it to social roles." I got carried away with my idea and suggested that by doing this we can actually create different social types, stating that we can even come up with new terms and call one of them "men" and the other "women"!

"Mmmm, and in your world, who would men be, and what would women be?" he asked me, puzzled with my idea.

"Why did you choose these terms in the first place? What do they mean?"

I had thought about this before. I admit that I chose the terms men and women randomly for no reason. I wanted the social types of males and females to have different terms than the biological one. But like female is a male with the prefix "fe," I came up with the word man and added the prefix "wo" to make it a woman.

"Females would be the men in that world, and they would be the ones working and striving for their livelihood just like shorts do in our world. Males would be the women, comfortable in homes, like our talls," I initially suggested.

"What are you talking about?!" he looked puzzled. He burst into laughter, then objected to my division of social roles, saying, "No, no, and no! I don't like your world at all."

"I am a male and I lived my entire life playing the role of a tall, which meant I had to stay home without working. If you are to imagine a different world, then you have to change the roles and have males be the men who work outside, and females be the women who stay home."

"Mmmm, okay then, as you wish!" I agreed as I couldn't let him down. "Males will be the men of that world."

I realized that he was right. I only wanted to imagine this new world to give males social advantages, honoring him. I got carried away in excitement, grabbed the book he was reading, pointed to its title and suggested sarcastically, "We can even write a new book with the title of *Men Are from Mars, Women Are from Venus.*"

He seemed intrigued, but after a moment of thinking he asked me, "What about intersex?"

"We would hide them under clothes to resemble one of the two types."

"Just like I do?" He responded with a hint of resentment. "That would be unfair to them!"

Again, he was right, but it was an injustice I could live with, in my imagination, as it carried a form of reparation for him. Through it, there was compensation for the life he had lived. Even if it was unjust to others, it gave him the status and image he deserved.

I smiled, telling myself that Tallan would be a Man in that world. And in my imagination, I started giving him all the manly attributes.

All of them!

29

I Carried My Promise to Tallan
as a Weapon on My Shoulder

I coughed a lot the morning we headed toward Willow's family house to ask for her hand in marriage. The cough intensified that night and became more frequent and worrying. I had a fit in the bathroom while washing my mouth. It was stronger than usual, to the extent that I felt something pressing on my chest, preventing me from breathing. I tried to throw up but failed. Red phlegm came out, filling the sink. I saw it with my eyes, but I didn't want to acknowledge what was happening.

Memories from my childhood returned to me, memories of my mother's last days when she couldn't stop coughing. I remembered how her way of walking changed, how her movement became slower, and how her body became thin and frail. Is history repeating itself? I felt chills in my veins. Was I following her path?

The implications of that thought scared me. I wanted to shout out, "NO!" I am not ready. I am not prepared to face this disease after meeting Tallan, gathering my loved ones, and creating a sort of family.

I looked in the mirror again, pressing my cheeks to ensure I hadn't lost weight. In my mind, I revisited a dream from weeks ago where I saw myself frail and light in front of Tallan, who took me in his arms and hugged me. I couldn't interpret the dream then. I thought it signified the death of the queen. But today, I feared it might be a prophecy. I shook off that image from my mind. I brushed away those fears and continued washing my face. I had to pull myself together for today. There were obligations and many things to arrange. No time for illusions.

Tallan was waiting for me to help him prepare for the delegation and to ensure he was ready to play his role seamlessly without any wrong gestures that might reveal his real identity. Moreover, Rocky hadn't arrived yet, and I needed to ensure her attendance to lead us.

I was worried she might cancel last minute after the serious argument I had with her last week. I had to tell her the whole truth about what has been going on in my life and I bluntly unveiled my relationship with Tallan to her. That faceoff wasn't pretty, but I was determined. I made up my mind and carried my promise to Tallan as a weapon on my shoulder when I decided to confront her. I wanted not only for her to accept Tallan's condition and challenge what she saw as a non-negotiable anomaly, but also to tell her the truth about Miles's same-height attraction, as well as his relationship with Willow, and Willow's pregnancy. I had to convince her to participate in this play and lead our delegation, knowing that playing this role in these circumstances contradicted her principles, morals, and beliefs. At the same time, I did not intend to condone what happened between her and Ray, or tone down my opposition to her using violence with her spouses.

Rocky, on the other hand, was waiting for me with much to say as well. She seized the chance of my arrival to complain about Ray's constant provocation and the drama Ray created every day. As I heard her speak, I sensed something was different about her this time. She had always been jealous over her spouses, and I knew all of her past stories along with all the quarrels she got herself into because of her jealousy and protective nature. She was never at ease when Ray or Pole had any interaction with a short, be it a family member or a stranger. But on that day, it seemed to me that her jealousy had turned into an obsession.

I could not believe my ears when she claimed, with confidence and much anger, that Pole, not Ray, was cheating on her with another short. She couldn't identify who might be the short or pinpoint a couple of suspects, but she was sure of what she said.

I gasped, my hips jolted, and my chest leaped from its place in the shock's intensity. I coughed violently, almost choking, before I found my voice to warn her about what she was claiming. "Rocky! This is a serious accusation. It cannot be casually thrown without substantial evidence."

"I know, I know," she replied seriously. "I assure you that I won't take any action until I find evidence. I'll find it soon. I know what I'm saying because his behavior and his coldness toward me in the last few months, before the incident with Ray and after it, all indicate that there's something else going on in his life."

Despite the seriousness of her words, I didn't want to believe her. I wouldn't have doubted the matter if she were accusing Ray of betrayal, but she was pointing at Pole, the beautiful, peaceful, gentle Pole, the loving and committed father. I didn't have time to engage in these disputes. I had a lot at stake. However, at that moment, I realized that I had to play along to succeed in the mission I came for. So, I found myself once again drawn into her world, agreeing with words I didn't find true, logical, or rational.

I held her hand and reiterated that she was a dear sister to me. "I am confident Pole is not cheating on you but if it turns out he is cheating, I will be here for you as a friend and as a sister and you have my full support."

She looked at me gratefully and thanked me for my encouraging words. But then, in a surge of anger, she bit her finger hard and threatened loudly, "I will kill him and drink his blood if he is betraying me."

I decided to change the topic. I used this opportunity of closeness to confide in her. "Rocky, I have a problem and need your help. I know what I'm going to ask might contradict your principles and morals, but I consider you my most trusted ally in this world, and I know your chivalry in tough situations."

I could see her calming down and looking at me curiously. Her body language changed as she became interested and less agitated. I asked her to sit down and listen to the whole story from the beginning to the end.

I first asked her if she had noticed the short that was sitting at the end of the dining room when she visited me the day Ray ran away from her house. She noticed him but didn't know who he was. Her mouth dropped in surprise after I informed her that he was the same tall who knocked on my door a few months ago.

"Oh my God, what happened to him? How did he change so much?" she gasped, looking shocked. She mentioned that she saw a resemblance between them, but her mind didn't connect the dots to conclude they were the same person. She noticed a vertical henna line on his forehead but didn't focus on it and convinced herself she must have been mistaken.

From that point, I started explaining everything that happened and how my relationship with Tallan had developed. It made her feel I trusted her to understand what I was saying.

"I knew you fell in love with him and wouldn't abandon him," she suddenly commented, reflecting her understanding of how weak I become when I fall in love.

"Is that why you claimed to have been ill?"

It was obvious so I didn't deny it. I admitted lying and apologized to her. I explained the challenges during that period and told her about the assault of which Tallan was a victim and how I had to go search for him and was forced to bring him to my house to care for him.

The story of the assault moved her. She got upset and cursed the perpetrators.

"Weren't they arrested?" she asked me.

I replied negatively.

"Isn't there a law in this country?"

"There are laws but they don't recognize the rights of mediums and don't protect or advocate for them," I responded.

She knew this fact very well and could not deny it. She was compassionate enough to agree that Tallan's medium height was a biological condition he didn't choose and that her belief in him being cursed did not justify any form of assault on him.

When I found initial agreement between her and me, I transitioned to the second part of the story, where I shocked her by the revelation about Miles's attraction to talls.

"What are you saying? What is this nonsense?" Her anger turned toward me as if I had told her that I have the desire for people of same-height, not him. At that moment, I excused her, as Miles was a distant relative of hers, and she had known him and his family for a long time. It was difficult for her to comprehend what I had just told her.

"Have you lost your mind?" she accused me.

I was aware of her thinking process and knew we had different moral compasses. Each of us was fully aware of the other's stance and was not content with it. We usually overlooked our differences to maintain our friendship and love for each other. However, today's debate was more intense than usual. I had to push from my side as much as I could. I knew she must have thought I influenced Miles and diverted him from his natural inclinations, though she didn't express it outright. She probably believed that, with my loose morals, I had convinced him to practice what's unnatural or unacceptable.

I had to correct her perception. I tried hard at that moment, but she wouldn't be convinced by my words. She wasn't willing to accept Miles's love for talls the way she accepted Tallan being a medium. Her point of view was that if both were considered deviant, then Tallan's situation couldn't be fixed. Miles, on the other hand, was willingly making this choice.

"Why does he insist on angering the gods by having a relationship with a person of similar height?' she repeated commonly held beliefs.

"How do you know what angers the gods and what doesn't?" I sharply responded, aware that she wouldn't be silenced. She would come back with inherited arguments and claims that were unquantifiable.

"Any relationship with two people of similar height is an immoral act." She quoted from the sacred books to convince me that her words were the absolute truth that shouldn't be debated. I was convinced that our argument was fruitless, so I decided to cut it short and confront her with reality. "Rocky, you have your beliefs, and I have mine. I cannot change your mind just as you cannot change mine. I consider Miles a member of my family and you consider him part of your family, too. You may not agree with his actions, but today, he is in a difficult situation."

I paused for a moment before clearly telling her, "His lover is pregnant. If the pregnancy becomes visible, you know very well the consequences."

I laid all the cards on the table clearly. She opened her mouth in shock.

I told her that his lover was as tall as him and that the only solution I thought of to get Miles out of his crisis was to have Tallan marry Willow before her pregnancy became noticeable.

I only approached her that day to ask for her help to complete the mission and to lead the delegation to ask for Willow's hand in marriage.

I made that clear.

30

Playing a Role I Hated
and Wasn't Good at

Rocky arrived after a slight delay. Any enthusiasm for the task I entrusted her with was missing but that didn't matter. Her presence was needed. We depended on her because she was the most suitable for this role. She was the best among us at steering the conversation with a group of shorts in a conservative environment that clings to traditions and norms. I, on the other hand, never liked the role of mediator. I have had a tendency to rebel, critique, and challenge the status quo since childhood. I have always had a strange love for everything new and unfamiliar.

Just a glance at Rocky from a distance was enough to reassure me of her ability to lead this group. Her formal attire, the golden threads of her robe, the long leather shoes, and the grand red turban on her thick hair, which all shorts must wear for this type of occasion, made her look authoritative. It was the only occasion where shorts are asked to lift their hair and conceal it.

Tallan looked similar when he stepped out of his room. Like Rocky, he wore a formal dark green robe, a red turban that hid part of his medium height, and flat leather shoes. With the red turban on, he didn't need to bend his back when he walked or use a cushion to create the illusion of a natural hump on his back. Not being very short, he may not have seemed conventionally handsome, but that didn't matter either. The name and wealth of his family were enough to convince Willow's family to accept his height, which seemed "close to average."

What mattered was that no one would dare claim he was deviant in any way, especially with the golden horizontal henna line on his forehead, replacing the vertical line I spent all of last night trying to cover up with makeup.

I looked similar to them in my dark gown, red turban, and leather shoes. We looked like any three proud shorts. Two of Tallan's cousins, both shorts, joined us, making our group complete with adequate social weight.

Miles was in the kitchen upon people's arrival, to make coffee for the short guests. I had to take over the task of distributing the coffee, as talls were not allowed in these circles. That made me sad since this was a proposal for his marriage and it should be all about him and Willow, not about Rocky and me!

Willow too was hiding in the kitchen behind the curtains when we arrived. She and her tall cousins prepared coffee and refreshing drinks for our shorts as the two groups joined.

Rocky took the lead in the gathering, sitting in the central seat as required, with me on her right and Tallan on her left. The rest of our shorts gathered around us, while their shorts sat opposite us on the other side of the room. She introduced herself, her family, their social status, and their long-standing presence in the country. She then introduced Tallan and his cousins, emphasizing the prestige of his family and their social and political influence. Following that, she discussed social customs and the significance of marriage as a sacred bond that unites talls and shorts, forming the fundamental structure of society, before delving into the main topic and requesting Willow's hand in marriage for Tallan.

Willow's short father responded by emphasizing the importance of customs and traditions, giving a brief history of his family, asking a few formal questions about Tallan, and then lifting his coffee cup as a sign of acceptance.

We held our hands together, raising them to symbolize the two families coming together through this sacred bond. Prayers were recited to celebrate the occasion.

Before we concluded the gathering, there was a small task I needed to accomplish. We had to hurry in arranging the wedding ceremony before pregnancy appeared on Willow. So, I moved and sat beside her father and told him about Tallan's wish to hold the ceremony as soon as possible. I claimed that one of Tallan's cousins would be leaving the city in ten days, and since he is close to Tallan, Tallan wished for the wedding to occur before his cousin's departure.

Fortunately, her father had no objections.

He agreed immediately, indicating the successful completion of our mission.

31

A Language That Would Introduce Tallan from a Different Dimension

Despite my exhaustion, the feeling of shortness of breath, and continuous struggles, I continued to work on designing a dress for Tallan for his wedding night. I wanted it to be magnificent, different from traditional festive clothing, but not so much so that its uniqueness would be off-putting to the guests.

It had to be daring, as that was what my designs were known for, but within reasonable limits.

In my mind, there was a revolutionary design concept I had wanted to try for a while. I had drawn it on paper but never dared to implement it before. A design that merges the usual robe with the underpants that are separate at the legs. It would have two openings, one for each leg, and would be different from underpants as it is wider. From a distance, it would look like regular clothing; a viewer wouldn't be able to see the separation of the legs. At the same time, it would give the thighs a greater prominence and show a certain bulkiness in the rear, adding elegance and highlighting its robustness.

This is what Tallan needed to somewhat compensate for his height, which would still appear to be close to average. His body measurements had changed since the last time, so it was easier to work with them to make a dress for a short groom. But while working on the suit and imagining how Tallan would look, I couldn't resist delving into my imagination, exploring this parallel world I had begun to outline.

As I imagined before, the basis of this world will be two main social types of human beings who are divided by sexual organs. This division determines other traits. Social roles will be clearly distributed and assigned to each social type, like they are divided and distributed among shorts and talls in our societies. As a tribute to Tallan and compensating for what he had to see in his life, and as I had previously agreed with him, this world will give social advantages to males in the same way we give our shorts. And as he requested, adult males with specific traits and social roles will be called men. They will be the ones having to work to support their families. On the other hand, adult females with opposing traits and roles will be called women. They will have to stay home and take care of their families.

With my imagination running wild for this world, the first thing that came to mind was the form and physique of these two social types and the imagery of their attire. It would work well if I exaggerated their imposing sexual organs' differences when designing their clothing.

I initially imagined them wearing garments similar to ours but with different colors; pristine white for men, complementing Tallan's dark skin, contrasted by black dresses for women, to match my taste and love for dark hues. Later on, my imagination ran wild as I worked on a wedding dress for Tallan. With the design of the underpants in the form of a wide dress with two openings for the legs, I imagined it to be a separate piece from the upper part of the dress and narrower than usual underpants. It resembled traditional underpants, but was more slender and made of better fabric. I designed it to suit men as it narrowed around the waist in a way that somewhat accentuated their lower genitalia.

I named it pants.

On the other hand, I envisioned a design for the upper part of the dress that narrows at the chest to emphasize upper genitalia of the females of that world. After several failed attempts, I succeeded in drawing a design inspired by the chest harness worn by our shorts to accommodate their large breasts. I modified it to accentuate the beauty of female breasts, making them appear more rounded, curvaceous, and alluring.

I named it bra.

I tried to see that world more clearly. I pondered the qualities suitable for women and those suitable for men but then I faced a language dilemma. How can the division built on the differences of the sexual organs in that world be reinforced without a language to establish and ground it? We know that in our world, our language evolved to base its structure on height. Our words have height connotations to indicate their short or tall nature. This is evident in our pronouns and many nouns that are linked to height in one way or another. Hence, the idea of creating a new language to complement the image of that world emerged: A language that would introduce Tallan from a different dimension, from a skewed angle that redistributed the balance of power among us. A language that is fairer and more equitable to him. A language where I am perceived as a female first, not as a short, and Tallan is celebrated as a male, not rejected as a medium.

I didn't start working on it until after Tallan's departure, and once I was certain that my days on this earth were numbered. It took me months to understand its nuances and its rules. I worked hard to master it so I could write this story with it: The story which I leave in your hands as a testament to our forbidden love.

In this language, words in relation to people must be linked to their genitalia, in a similar way to our words, which are linked to our height. I had to find new terms to refer to family members and certain occupations in order to solidify this sex division in the mind of every speaker of this language, just as the height division is ingrained in us. I made sure to use the word "man" instead of "short" before neutral terms we use to refer to everyone, such as *shortkind*, *shortpower*, and *shortmade*, making them *mankind*, *manpower,* and *manmade.* And since the word *short* was the base we used to refer to all of our kind by saying *hushort*, I replaced it with *man*, and made *human*.

To make things easier for myself, I started with pronouns, and made up alternatives for personal pronouns, demonstrative pronouns, possessive pronouns, and reflexive pronouns. I wanted to make sure that whenever I referred to someone in this language, their sex was hinted at.

I followed that by creating a table for words as a code to help me write in this language. I listed all the words I counted in our language and their equivalents in the new language. I followed simple rules to convert each word with height connotation to be suitable for the new gender-based language as following:

- Words that were not linked to height stayed the same, untampered.
- Words of family members linked to being short: I replaced their first letter from S to a random letter.
- Words of family members linked to being tall: I replaced their first letter from T to a random letter.
- Words of occupations linked to being short: I replaced the part that mentions short with man, and kept man at the end of the word. For example: *shortpolice* became *policeman*.
- Words of occupations linked to being tall: I replaced the part that mentions tall with woman, and kept woman at the end of the word. For example: *tallcrafts* became *craftswoman*.
- In certain words that refer to occupations with a suffix at the end of the word to refer to talls, such as the word *actor* which typically refers to a short actor, and its tall counterpart that refers to a tall actor *actrell*, I kept the short part of the word as it

is for men, and replaced the last two letters for the
talls, so the two Ls tailing the word became two Ss,
and *actrell* became *actress*.

I did everything needed to complete this language as
a mirror of our own. A linguistic mirror that reflected
its tall polarity onto females and its short polarity onto
males. A language that can be used to shape an alternate
world in which I want to be reborn and live a happier life
with my lover Tallan.

To finalize the image of this new world, I went beyond establishing the basis of its language and setting
the physical division of its humans to be gender based. I
reshaped its genetic makeup. I rewrote it to suit the new
world, to eliminate any alleged doubt that the division of
human beings should be based on sex, not height.

My line of thought was the following:

All of us are taught that the human genetic code con-
sists of twenty-three pairs of chromosomes, twenty-two
pairs of which are shared between shorts and talls, in addition to the last pair, named the *height pair*. This height
pair carries identical chromosomes in shorts but different
ones in talls. The match of these chromosomes in shorts
confirms the presence of two copies of the short gene that
limits one's height. Their difference in talls denotes only
one gene for limiting height, thus losing the robustness of
talls' bodies as they grow taller. No one mentioned that
the same pair of chromosomes we refer to as height pair,
also carries genes that determine the sex of an individual.

If we wanted to identify this pair of chromosomes with one trait, why didn't we choose to identify based on genes related to sex, calling them sex chromosomes instead of height chromosomes?

I did my research and came to conclude that most females carry identical chromosomes, while most males carry different ones. This in itself explains the differentiation in sexual organs, as the male lacks the gene set required to form the uterus and the completion of female sexual organs, which results in his body releasing his testicles from their sockets inside the body and enlarging his reproductive organs.

Therefore, I decided to retain the symbols used to represent this last pair of chromosomes but redefine it to consolidate the division based on sex.

"X" will no long express shorts; instead it will point to females.

"Y" will not be the talls' identifier chromosome; it will indicate maleness.

Thus, the picture was almost finalized. There was no longer room for skepticism about the existence of two human types divided by sex, just as the picture is nearly complete in our world where no one doubts the existence of two human types divided by height.

32

Revolution

One does not realize the fragility of life until fate grasps him and takes away everything he knows in this world, all pleasures and sorrows, all fears and anxieties, all plans and dreams.

That ominous day, right before Tallan's wedding night, caught us off guard while we were gathered in the café where I first met Willow. We were chatting, planning to enjoy the fake wedding night, laughing at our ability to deceive people around us just as they deceived and marginalized us and deprived us of our most basic human rights; our right to love whomever we choose, our right to bodily sovereignty, and our right to express ourselves the way we want.

Had that wedding taken place as planned, I would have danced all night, cheered loudly without embarrassment, and welcomed the guests passionately as if it were my own wedding. I would have been so happy to see Tallan celebrated among the crowds. With me standing by his side, protecting him from anyone who might dare ask about his true height. Clapping for him as he danced the shorts' dance, perfectly in sync with their movements, chubby, grounded, dignified, and steadfast.

At the end of the night, after the ceremony and his return with his bride to my house, I would have stolen him from Willow, leaving her in the arms of Miles. I would lead Tallan to my room to celebrate our love, thank him for completing the mission, and spend the night with him until dawn, as if it were my wedding night, not Willow's.

But none of that happened.

I couldn't believe my ears when I heard those loud chants from talls' crowds outside. I didn't comprehend what was happening, even when Celestia approached us excitedly, raising her fist in the air and repeatedly shouting "Revolution! Revolution!"

Revolution? Revolution? What revolution was she talking about? We were perplexed by her words and signaled her for clarification. We didn't understand what she meant by "the talls' revolution" until after we left the café and ran outside through its hidden corridor, only to be surprised by the crowds.

They came from every direction toward the city center by the Great River. Diverse groups of talls in huge numbers I had never seen before, angry and chanting bold revolutionary slogans.

"We won't be silenced anymore."

"There are no differences between shorts and talls."

"We won't tolerate shorts' crimes anymore."

We joined them without thinking. Our small group consisting of me, Tallan, Miles, Willow, Celestia, and several others who resembled us and had come out of the café behind us, all talls and shorts and in-betweens, formed a diverse group that crossed height boundaries and shouted in one voice in favor of talls' liberation.

Who started this revolution, I wondered! I was curious to know what had stirred the masses' anger and driven them out of their homes, defying constraints, customs, and social boundaries that had defined their relationship with shorts for decades.

What had pushed talls to revolt? I wanted to know, and I wish I hadn't! I wish I hadn't seen that day!

Amid the chants demanding legal protection for talls and other rights they had longed for, and among other specific chants calling for retribution and punishment for a certain murderer, I learned the painful truth.

A heinous crime occurred yesterday.

One of the shorts assaulted her tall spouse violently, resulting in severe injuries and a laceration to the liver. The spouse was admitted to the hospital last night but a few hours after entering the hospital, he passed away due to the injuries.

The headline on the cover of the city's newspaper read in bold:

An Act of Rage Takes the Life of a Tall

The headline was accompanied by a photo of the victim, his face bloodied, as he was rushed into the emergency room at the hospital. His features were not visible due to the bruises and disfigurements on his face. A brief caption about the crime was written beneath the photo, but the details and the full name of the victim, as well as the murderer's photo, were mentioned inside. I immediately rushed to check it, only to get the shock of my life.

I felt dizzy like never before as I recognized her immediately! "No, Rocky, no!" I exclaimed hysterically. "What have you done, my dear? What have you done, you crazy?"

I was on the verge of losing my mind, unable to believe what my eyes were seeing. How could she kill her spouse? How could I forgive myself for thinking Rocky could never do such a thing?

"Pole," I read the victim's name and was immediately devastated.

I was confused.

It couldn't be Pole who was killed.

How is it possible for someone like him, so calm, loyal, loving, and endearing, to meet such a gruesome end?

I looked at the front page to confirm he was the victim. Part of me was hoping that it was Ray, not him. But the moment I saw the picture again, I realized it was him. I broke down, crying and wailing. I remembered Rocky's explicit words, her wild suspicions about him, her biting her finger in anger, and her clear threat to kill him if her suspicions were confirmed. "I will kill him and drink his blood if he's cheating on me"—those were her exact words.

Back then, I neither believed Pole could betray her nor did I take her threats seriously. I thought she was exaggerating and creating something out of nothing.

Alas! I was wrong.

I read the details of the crime to understand what happened. It was written in a way to exonerate Rocky from responsibility, casting doubt on Pole's actions and character while justifying her horrendous act. Even though the police detained her for questioning, the evidence pointed to a fit of rage that made her lose control and commit the crime. She claimed that seeing Pole in public with another short made her lose her mind.

This was expected in the collective consciousness as a natural reaction for any quick-tempered short who perceives a threat to his family or betrayal from his spouse. Everyone knows, without doubt, that shorts, by nature, were quick to react, and their instinct to protect their families was a fundamental trait instilled in each of them. Therefore, the law reflected this reality, exempting them from punishment for crimes deemed beyond their control. With Rocky's pregnancy, public opinion would easily sway in her favor. The police might release her immediately after the investigation as if nothing happened, or impose house arrest on her for several months as a punishment.

The masses of talls weren't satisfied with that. Angry, they protested in a unified voice, demanding the harshest punishment for the criminal—Rocky, my friend. I didn't know how to act amid all this hysteria. Had Rocky not been the perpetrator or had another been the criminal, I would have joined their demands. I would have raised my voice like them, demanding a change in the law, justice for the victim, and punishment for the criminal. However, I couldn't do that on that day, even if it contradicted my principles and values, as we were talking about a lifelong friend.

I hurried toward Tallan, informed him of the reality of what happened, and told him about the real reason behind the anger of these crowds. He was holding the newspaper in his hand and seemed to have already understood what had happened. He surprised me by approaching me, hugging me, and comforting me. I expected him to scold me because he had warned me earlier that something like this might happen, but he didn't utter a word. He seemed angry at Rocky and what she had done but he was aware of my awkward position at the same time. However, when I gathered my courage and asked him to accompany me and go to the police station to support Rocky, his facial expression changed. He looked at me bewildered. "What are you saying?" he exclaimed, rising and raising his hands as if to fend me off and keep me away. "I won't leave this place!

"You can't do anything now," he warned me. "You can sympathize with her as you like but you can't justify the crime she committed or defend her and support her to escape its consequences."

I wouldn't listen to him no matter what he said, no matter how angry he became. I wanted to leave immediately as I wouldn't want to join a revolution that demands the death penalty for my friend. I couldn't bear to see someone I loved deeply participating in it and supporting their demands either.

I looked for Miles, hoping he could rescue me. He was familiar with Rocky's situation, and perhaps his stance would be milder than Tallan's. But he, too, refused to leave.

"This revolution doesn't target Rocky alone but the entire social system that favors shorts. The system that pushes the likes of her to become murderers without any repercussions or punishments," Miles claimed in a confident voice as if he were a lawyer presenting a case.

"How does it not target her?!" I exclaimed. "How is she not targeted when the chants are filled with her name, repeating the demands for her execution?"

I understood Tallan's position, but I couldn't comprehend Miles's stance. How could he behave this way after Rocky stood up for him? After she set aside her opinions on his love for Willow and agreed to lead the delegation of Tallan's marriage proposal? Did what she could to save Willow from a fate similar to what Pole faced?

"How can you abandon Rocky after she stood by you in your time of need?" I asked.

He didn't change his opinion. He expressed gratitude for her assistance and for standing by him during his ordeal but added that this didn't negate the fact that she committed the crime. It didn't change the reality of laws that protect these crimes, or the fact that he, his lover, and their child are easy targets for such crimes without any protection. The uprising was an opportunity for him. An opportunity to rise, to raise his voice, and to demand justice for himself. An opportunity to lay a foundation for the future he wants his child to live in.

I failed to persuade them. I couldn't stay with them either. I let them join the crowds, and watched them disappear between them, my heart heavy with sadness. I retreated, trying to think of a way to find Rocky.

Reaching the city center, where the police station was located, via the main bridge seemed nearly impossible with these crowds. I needed to find an alternate route using one of the smaller side bridges.

No sooner had I moved away to find my way than I heard shouting and wailing. I turned toward the source and saw talls in uproar, scrambling chaotically and panicking. From a distance, I saw several bulky shorts appearing on top of the bridge. They were holding rocks of various sizes and hurling them at talls.

No one expected this!

Talls had no choice but to run, trying to escape rocks by distancing themselves from the bridge as much as possible or hiding behind a tree or under some surface. Since they were in an open space, there were few surfaces to hide under or trees to hide behind. Some were hit, some fell, and some screamed in panic. Blood filled the square. The chants calling for justice and equality turned into a horrific massacre unlike anything the city had seen before.

I retraced my steps and headed toward the crowds, looking for Tallan and Miles. I ran, trying to avoid the rush of the masses of talls in the opposite direction, raising my arm high as a peace sign so that they wouldn't mistake me for one of those shorts who attacked them.

Rushing toward the center of the tumult where the stones were falling was tantamount to suicide, but I was afraid that Tallan might be there among the talls near the bridge. I trembled at the thought of him being hit by one of those stones, so I decided to take a side path to find an elevated place at the foot of the mountain where I could stand and search for him.

From my vantage point, I saw some talls, after recovering from the shock, organizing themselves and taking cover behind some trees. They were carrying stones in their turn and retaliating against the attacking group of shorts. I found a side passage on my way leading to a stack of rocks between a clump of grass and trees outside the rock. I decided to climb it to search for Tallan. I clung to it with difficulty, trying to lift my heavy body to move to the top. I almost slipped and fell but I maintained my balance and ascended slowly. Once I could carry myself and stood on that elevation, I looked carefully toward the crowd center. There I spotted Tallan with his distinctive green robe among the masses of talls.

He seemed agitated, taking cover behind a large tree, blending with a group of talls near him, collecting stones to take turns and launch them toward the shorts. I called out to him, but he couldn't hear me from that distance. I looked to my right, and from my elevated position I noticed other groups of shorts beginning to appear in elevated side areas on the edges of the mountain. Some were standing in place, throwing stones, while others gathered, holding sticks and weapons, heading with hostility down the mountain to confront and disperse them.

I tried to alert Tallan by shouting his name at the top of my voice in hopes he would hear me. I didn't care about the flying rocks, or the coughing fit that overcame me as I screamed in panic. I didn't care about the impending danger from the other groups of shorts approaching. I lost my mind and ran toward the crowds, trying to reach him despite my heavy weight. I pushed through the crowds obstructing my path, making it harder to get to him. Beside me, shouts and wails grew louder, with talls falling one after the other without help or rescue from anyone.

I was too late.

Delayed for moments I swear I would trade my life for.

Those few moments separated me from saving the one I loved most in this world.

I approached him as he finally noticed my screams and felt my presence. He looked at me with a glance that assured me he was grateful for my return. I read in his eyes a profound fear for me and my being in that turmoil. Maybe he wanted to rush to take my hand and guide me to safety behind the tree. I saw him let his guard down and step toward me. But as he took a step, I saw him stagger in front of me, losing his balance with a burst of blood from his head, covering all his face.

I screamed in terror as I saw a large sharp stone hit him from behind.

I rushed to him, trying to get to him before he fell. I caught him in my arms as he collapsed, drenched in his blood. I pulled out a handkerchief from my pocket and wiped his head, trying to apply pressure to the wound. Panicking, I shouted for help, asking if there was a doctor among the crowd. I didn't expect to find one, because only shorts were allowed to become doctors. Fortunately, one of the talls responded that his short spouse was a doctor and that he had trained him in basic first aid. He guided me to keep pressing the wound. He asked me to keep talking to Tallan so he wouldn't lose consciousness and then inquired if anyone had water. He took some to wipe Tallan's face.

Things took a turn a moment later as the gangs of shorts reached our area and started to brutally beat the talls as if they were in a state of war. They decided to take the law into their own hands, punishing talls for daring to demand justice and equality. Lawless gangs that cared about nothing.

From my place, I couldn't stand idle and not intervene, even though they didn't target me. I got up when I saw one of them approach Willow, intending to hit her. I rushed toward him and hit him in the face with my fist, attacking him with all my might, knocking him to the ground.

"RUN, RUN," I urged her.

I saw Miles holding her hand, running away with her as shorts converged around me and began attacking from all sides. I tried to resist them initially, snatching a baton from one and knocking down another but they overwhelmed me. Their numbers were far greater than my ability to fend them off.

With their blows, I lost my balance and fell.

I couldn't fight anymore.

I lost consciousness.

33

I Felt an Unending Darkness

I heard knocking on the door. I knew it was Tallan. I rushed to open the door to greet him. I saw him standing with his usual smile, holding a jasmine flower as a reminder of the bouquets he once gave me. I extended my hand to take it and thanked him for his gesture. As soon as I grasped it, it vanished right before my eyes.

Startled and frightened, I looked at him, wanting to ask if he saw what happened, but he had also disappeared. I looked left and right searching for him. I couldn't find him. He vanished as if he wasn't there just a moment ago, as if I was imagining his presence.

I felt an unending darkness deep in my heart.

That dream repeated itself every night. Tallan visited me, sometimes appearing as a tall, sometimes disguised as a short. At times, he appeared in his recent shape, like he was in the last days of his life, a bulky short with long hair. I cherished every form and shape of him and eagerly anticipated each of these visits. I rushed to open the door to take the jasmine flower from his hand, only to be surprised by his sudden disappearance after greeting me. I was then overwhelmed by intense sadness. I woke up from my dream with mixed feelings; enveloped by warmth from seeing him and sensing his closeness, yet full of painful yearning to face the reality of his absence.

It was difficult to accept what happened. I wasn't ready to let go of the idea of his existence in my life. I clung to his presence and spent the months following his departure crafting the special world that I had begun sketching before he left.

It was a fateful day when Rocky killed Pole, the day masses of talls rose up, demanding retribution. If only we hadn't heard the chants of those crowds, and ignored the voice of Celestia when she arrived from a distance screaming to inform us about the revolution. If only I had held onto Tallan and had hidden him between my arms. If I had tried to dissuade him from leaving the corridor of that café and urged him to pull back before things spiraled out of control.

What were we thinking that day? Why did I let him join a futile revolution that lacked all the requirements for success? Did they want justice and equality? Were they demanding revenge for the short killer? Were they chanting for freedom from the tyranny of shorts? What did they achieve?

They recorded the voice of the first revolution in history bearing the signature of talls!

What does that mean? If it means anything at all! What about the price that was paid? What about Tallan, who never experienced a joyous day in his life? Tallan, whom I wished to compensate for what he missed? He did not have the chance to taste the sweetness of happiness.

The world denied him the joy of being loved by someone who didn't care about the curse of his average height.

What about the other talls? The many who lost their lives in this revolution, and the others who were badly hurt. Those whose eyes were gouged out, ribs crushed, and heads injured by rocks or batons. The rest who were dealt with by the shortpolice and were detained. And those whose families disapproved of their participation in the revolution and subjected them to even harsher abuse than the gangs of shorts.

The revolution failed. Yes, it failed like all revolutions that bloom prematurely. Revolutions that don't understand the dynamics of power, that aren't fortified with lethal weapons capable of seizing desired rights from their oppressors. Those naive revolutions where masses rise spontaneously and emotionally without enough fire to ignite the earth and its contents.

That day, they pulled me from the midst of the crowd, unconscious, to the emergency room for treatment. There, I regained consciousness. Immediately, I remembered what had happened and began crying for Tallan.

As if I felt he was gone.

I needed to verify that. In a frenzy, I jumped off the examination bed, pushed the nurse aside, and ran through the corridors calling him. I searched for him in the faces of the patients. My heart would race every time I saw an injured short, thinking it might be him. I saw him several times in the form of a short walking near me. As I rushed toward the short, calling them Tallan, I grabbed their face, turning it toward me. I saw their features and got disappointed when I realized it wasn't him. I then left the short and distanced myself from them, leaving them looking at me puzzled and wondering about my foolishness.

Oh, the irony! Tallan died as a short after living his life as a tall. He passed away fighting for justice he didn't get to experience, playing a role that wasn't his and bearing a physique that wasn't his own.

By the time he was brought into the emergency room on a stretcher, he was already gone. He was deaf to my screams as I wrestled with the nurses and clung to him, hugging him, kneeling, pleading with him not to leave, not to leave me here without him. When he remained silent, anger surged within me. I found myself gripping the stretcher tightly, shaking it to prevent the nurses from pulling it, yelling at him, "Come back, come back, I won't let you abandon me."

I only let him go when several nurses gathered and restrained my hands, overpowering me and limiting my movement.

Tallan left and didn't come back.

He only returned in those precious moments when he visited me in my dreams. He wasn't the only one who left me that day. Miles took his beloved and left too. He wasn't at home when I returned the next morning. He left me a farewell note, thanking me for all I had done for him and apologizing for his sudden departure. He wrote of the revolution's failure, our shattered dreams, and his despair over our inability to bring about the desired change. He expressed his grief over everything we lost that day and explained his need, along with Willow, to take control of their lives, to protect themselves and their child from what might happen now after Tallan's death. They quickly left the city that night amid all the chaos without saying a proper goodbye to anyone.

Given what transpired, they had no other option. They left me alone, so lonely, trying to comprehend the darkness that engulfed me. Grieving, I was incapable of performing any ordinary daily tasks. I could only sit for hours and hours. I would imagine hearing their voices and smelling their scents. I gave in to long bouts of crying and sobbing until I lost my strength and succumbed to sleep.

It had been two weeks since all this happened when Rocky unexpectedly visited me.

I was sitting alone in the sewing room, lost in melancholy when I noticed her. It felt like I saw a ghost because she was the last person I expected to see. I was not prepared to face my emotions toward her. At that moment, I only felt immense anger toward her, like I had never felt before. I left her for a moment, hoping that she would be a figment of my imagination that disappears when my sanity returns. However, she didn't vanish but started talking. She greeted me with a good morning as if nothing had happened, as if we were living one of those ordinary days when she used to come in the morning to greet me and start her work.

I looked at her for a long moment before I gathered myself to speak, cutting off her words, and asked her in disbelief, "How did you get out of jail so quickly?" I didn't give her a chance to respond. Without any warning I stood up and lifted one of the lightweight chairs in my hands. I called her a criminal and waved the chair in front of her before striking her with it.

"What's wrong with you, are you crazy?" She grabbed the chair in fear before it hit her protruding belly. She surprised me with her ability to resist my attack despite the heaviness of her burden.

I continued my assault without responding to her.

After a struggle, she managed to overturn the chair from my hands, but that only fueled my anger. I found myself attacking her with all my strength, pushing her backward with my massive arms. She didn't expect it. Although she tried to step back to recover from the assault and regain her balance, she couldn't succeed. Slipping backward, her back collided violently with the ground. And because of my momentum, I couldn't maintain my balance, feeling myself falling on top of her with the weight of my body landing on her swollen belly.

She screamed in pain, afraid for her unborn child.

I wasn't myself that day. I wanted to punish her for what she did to Pole. I attacked her because she was responsible for Tallan's death. I attacked her because she pushed Miles and Willow to leave. I didn't stop when I heard her screams. I didn't care about her pleas as I raised my fists toward her face.

I continued my barrage of rapid, successive punches. Like a crazy short, I yelled in her face, "Is this the violence you want? Is this how you punish your partners? Is this how you lose your mind?"

I didn't stop until I saw the blood oozing from her nose and lips after I had bruised her cheeks and eyes. When I finally looked back at what I'd done, I wasn't sure whether I felt relieved or remorseful for my actions.

What truly horrified me was seeing the blood streaming between her legs as she held onto her stomach, sobbing.

I realized then that I had killed her child.

That made me sad.

34

What Matters to Me
Is for Tallan's Memory
to Be Cherished

I was horrified when I saw blood flowing between Rocky's legs. I didn't know how to react. I left her lying on the ground and rushed out of the house, seeking help from my neighbors who rushed to my aid. Fortunately, among them was a doctor who had recently moved to the neighborhood. He quickly came to help and tried to stabilize her. He checked her blood pressure and her heart rate. While he was trying to stop her bleeding, he asked me to keep talking to her and distract her to prevent her from fainting.

She screamed from the pain, holding her stomach as if she were in labor, fearful for her unborn child. With her fall and heavy bleeding, the risk to her child's life was significant, so the doctor ordered her immediate transfer to the hospital, where she and her baby's life were saved.

It truly was a miracle. A miracle that saved the child and saved me from living the rest of my days in this world with the guilt of killing an innocent child. Though I accompanied her to the hospital that day and did not leave her side until her condition stabilized, I did not go into her room to congratulate her on her safety. I wasn't prepared to face her after what had occurred. I wasn't ready for reconciliation, but I didn't leave without checking on the baby among premature babies in the intensive care unit. I stood there watching him through the glass. I felt Pole standing next to me, looking at his boy. I couldn't stop imagining his reaction had he been present at the birth of his child, seeing the beauty of his face. How proud and delighted he would have been of his second born.

He wasn't here. The poor man departed before his time, leaving behind both of his children to be raised amid the stubbornness of Rocky and her rigid thinking, as well as the arrogance, jealousy, and self-love of Ray. These poor kids would live in the same world that Pole experienced, growing up to embody one of the two human types, thin talls or fat shorts.

I couldn't bear this loathsome division anymore, especially after the dispute that arose during Tallan's funeral when there was a debate among short religious leaders, wondering about his height so that they could figure out how to conduct this funeral properly. How could they complete the final chapter of his life without a clear categorization? Would they scatter his ashes in the great river, as is done for the ashes of shorts after their cremation, or in the desert, as is the practice for talls? They adhered to what their books dictate, enabled by their gods exchanging human souls at the end of their lives, with the Great River god harvesting the souls of shorts and the Sun goddess reaping the souls of talls.

Tallan's soul remains undefined, rejected by the gods as their representatives on earth reject it. I felt utter despair when they all agreed that he didn't deserve cremation because the gods wouldn't be pleased with it. Instead, they recommended burying him intact, beneath the earth's surface, for worms to consume his body while his soul remains trapped between the two worlds. Cursed at birth and cursed long after his death.

With no recourse after the commands were given and no one daring to oppose, I returned that day to my home, feeling sad and severely ill. I vomited blood and swore to complete the picture of the world I had envisioned to make it more just for Tallan. I cursed those gods and damned their shorts, vowing to spend the remainder of my days in my imagined world.

I wanted to master the language I invented, and to write this story in a language that would glorify Tallan as a man, indifferent to the length of his body.

I remember telling myself, "If the gods of shorts and talls rejected him, then I reject them too." I will not believe in them anymore! What kind of foolish gods are these that let their children live with this injustice due to a body they did not choose? That foolish river with no soul and that blundering sun that's no different from the domestic fire I cook on. If there's a true god, it must be longer than this river and warmer than that sun. It must be a God without boundaries or limits, beyond the physical limits and human categorizations and divisions.

It won't be short or tall and it will have no rivals.

"He" will be ONE God, not two.

In my imagining of this God and writing about him in this new language, I made a conscious choice to refer to him as a masculine entity so that it is closer to the image of a male Tallan. I, deliberately, decided that the keys to power in this world will be in the hands of men, honoring Tallan. And hence, I created a patriarchal system where the older man in the family has absolute authority. I called him "father," followed by his female spouse called "wife," and a set of children. A system where God is at the top of the pyramid, followed by the father, then the male children according to age.

I will believe in this God instead of the river god and the sun goddess. I'll pray for him to protect my beloved Tallan from harm.

It took me months to complete my vision for this world and to outline my love story with Tallan from the moment he appeared at my door, where I was amazed by him, to being in a relationship with him, through the complete change of my awareness toward societal relationships and the inherited division of roles and identities that shape us. Ending with losing along with everyone I loved in this world and spending the last days of my life writing this story to document the last two years of my life.

During these months, my health progressively deteriorated. I lost a lot of weight, and I no longer felt like a short. I knew my days were numbered and my only consolation during these days was working on completing this story. I always comforted myself with my vision of a world where Tallan would be fully healthy and radiant. He would greet me, thanking me for designing a world where he is valued. He would open the door for me and welcome me as his wife and bride.

At times, I found myself wondering if the world I imagined was brighter and more just than our own.

I remembered Tallan's words when he objected to my idea when I presented it to him, "Why do we divide humans in the first place? Isn't it more appropriate for us to fight against the division, categorization, and discrimination among humans in all its types and forms?" Then, I realized that what I had worked on and envisioned was nothing but a mirror of the life I lived.

A mirror of our lives reflected on another axis would not be less ugly.

I might have been fair to Tallan, but I wronged myself and others who would not fit this new split. Any division of humans is flawed because it will create different categories, some of which will benefit, and others will be harmed. But how could the world be without any form of division? I didn't know, and I didn't have the strength to imagine it. All that matters to me is for Tallan to be cherished.

I handed these final words over to Celestia, the only one who visited and cared for me during my sick days. She had recently undergone surgery to lengthen her legs after the failed revolution, and achieved her dream of fitting her tall identity. She's much healthier now and can appear publicly without any awkwardness due to her unusual appearance and movement. Moreover, she recently met a short and fell in love. They're planning to get married soon.

I wish her happiness and, for all of you, a more just, tolerant, and loving society.

With love,
The Tailor

Afterword

Cheryl Toman

For some North American readers, *The Man of Middling Height* might be a first look into the literary universe of gender rights advocate Fadi Zaghmout, but in fact, this author's novels and blogs have been recognized and celebrated in the Arab world and in Europe for more than a decade. Not only is Zaghmout arguably the most important Jordanian writer today, but he has allowed a new generation of Jordanian voices to be heard in transnational and transcultural discussions about gender and sexuality. The author of five novels originally written in Arabic with some already available in translation in the United Kingdom, France, and Italy, Zaghmout infuses into his texts characters, settings, and contexts specific to the Arab world, but at the same time, he is speaking about universal issues and the struggle to overcome patriarchy and threats to one's freedom and existence due to rigid written and unwritten rules governing gender and how and whom one can love. *The Man of Middling Height* proves that Middle Eastern writers can and do convey messages to which all readers can relate.

Of course, Zaghmout is not the first novelist that Jordan has ever produced, but in a sense he stands alone. As in other national literatures of the Middle East, the majority of Jordanian authors have placed war and conflict at the core of their writings. It was through creating and writing blogs that Zaghmout came to the realization that young Jordanians—like youth in other Arab countries—were desperately seeking out platforms and literature that spoke to them about the issues that were most important to them and Zaghmout finally gave them what they had been looking for. While threats of war and conflict do weigh upon all of those living in the Middle East, a younger generation of Arabs have grown weary of the expectation that they are destined to carry their parents' historical baggage. Zaghmout arrived on the scene and fulfilled the need of a generation; he placed gender and sexuality at the center of his work and in doing so, he singlehandedly changed the face of Jordanian literature both within the country and beyond its borders. Zaghmout's novels and his media presence have at times forced a necessary conversation about taboos and oppressive elements of Jordanian society and the Arab world—a conversation that many were ready to have. Although his writings at times create heated debate in Jordan, Zaghmout has indeed opened a dialogue that will eventually lead to undoing the dehumanization of nonconforming and gender-fluid citizens of the Arab world.

Experts of Middle Eastern literature are well aware that in recent years, Lebanese authors have been some of the first to expose taboos pertaining to sexuality and gender. Female protagonists in cosmopolitan Beirut dominate novels like Sahar Mandour's *32* (2010, 2016) and Alexandra Chreiteh's *Always Coca-Cola* (2009, 2012), to cite just two prime examples. A bit earlier in 2005, Saudi writer Rajaa Alsanea also earned worldwide acclaim for touching upon similar issues in her novel, *Girls of Riyadh*. All of these works are available in English translation. In 2012, however, Zaghmout's *The Bride of Amman* complemented these works, showing readers that Jordanians, too, had much to say on this topic. But Zaghmout went a step further. Not only did he highlight female protagonists in his debut novel, but readers also empathized with gay characters who, despite the obstacles they face in their society, were presented in a positive light. Alexandra Chreiteh's second novel, *Ali and his Russian Mother* (2010, 2015) also introduced a positive portrait of a gay character, Ali, into contemporary Middle Eastern, but her portrayal was much more subtle and nuanced. Zaghmout's characters in *The Bride of Amman* brought issues clearly into the spotlight, and furthermore, all were navigating Jordanian society from the inside and not from the margins. Chreiteh's Ali realized he could not live in Lebanon and thus he becomes a visitor and an outsider in his own country. Although Zaghmout's characters do not always feel free in their society, there is no other "home" to which they can escape so they are determined to create their own local safe spaces.

In the Arab world especially, if not globally, social media has a potential to create a safe space for youth, an outlet for discussing taboos about sexuality and relationships that guarantees a certain anonymity in a virtual world where there are fewer rules and thus more freedom of expression. As technology advances at the speed of lightning, older generations have failed to keep up and to some extent, this reality has helped secure a space where Arab youth can express themselves far from the judgments and criticisms of their elders.

Fadi Zaghmout was born in 1978 in Amman, Jordan, and he has lived in the Arab world nearly his whole life, but his graduate work in creative writing at Sussex University in the United Kingdom also groomed him to become the prominent novelist he is today. His most widely read novel, *The Bride of Amman*, was actually published before embarking on this formal journey in creative writing. After earning his degree in England, he returned home to the Middle East; first back to Amman, and then to the United Arab Emirates. Zaghmout is a self-described feminist sexual freedoms and body rights advocate[1] who has been greatly inspired by pioneers like American scholar and philosopher Judith Butler and the late Egyptian essayist and novelist Nawal El Saadawi. But he is also internationally recognized for his work, contributing short stories to magazines and collections and receiving invitations to speak about his writing, and he

---

1. https://fadizaghmout.com.

is the recipient of the British Council's 2024 Study UK Social Action Award in the UAE.

It was after publishing *The Bride of Amman* that Zaghmout gravitated towards speculative fiction, and we see his evident passion for this genre in *The Man of Middling Height*. His first published science fiction novel from 2014, *Janna Ala Al Ard*, was translated by Sawad Hussein and published in English in 2017 as *Heaven on Earth*. This was followed by *Laila wal Hamal* in 2017, translated in 2020 by Hajer Almosleh into English as simply *Laila*. Zaghmout's fourth novel, *The Man of Middling Height*, first appeared in Arabic in late 2020 under the title *Ebra Wa Kushtuban* which literally translates as "a needle and a thimble." The futuristic novel *Amal Ala Al Ard* (Hope on Earth) is his fifth novel, published in 2023.

Readers of *The Man of Middling Height* can certainly understand the reference to the needle and the thimble pervasive in this novel—set in an alternate universe where people are discriminated against according to height and not gender. Zaghmout poignantly illustrates here the absurdity of one group in society dominating another and he mocks the arbitrary and nonsensical way in which we determine societal hierarchy. The image conveyed by a needle and a thimble is about complementarity, and when these two work together, as they do in sewing, something wonderful can result, as Zaghmout deftly explains in *The Man of Middling Height*: "What I learned in my younger years was that both the needle and the thimble are necessary; they complete each other's work. One cannot succeed without the other and together they can create almost anything. In this, I felt it was exactly like our social fabric. It cannot exist or function without the cooperation of both talls and shorts" (40).

Zaghmout's characters navigate urban society, and they are like hundreds of real people one can encounter in day-to-day interactions in cosmopolitan Middle Eastern cities such as Amman. But these protagonists are presented in a way that make them familiar to both Arab and non-Arab readers alike. Zaghmout achieves this through emphasizing the commonalities that all people have shared at some point in their lives when exploring questions pertaining to sexuality, feminisms, and masculinities, ideas which all contribute to shaping one's own identity in today's turbulent world. As relatable as Zaghmout's characters are in a novel such as *The Bride of Amman*, they are still unmistakably Jordanian and Zaghmout has effectively brought these voices into a conversation in which they had seemed absent before. However, how does one explain Zaghmout's fictional, parallel world in *The Man of Middling Height*? No country is ever identified outright in the novel even if certain nuances lead readers to believe that the setting was inspired by the Arab world. But this is exactly what makes *The Man of Middling Height* so original. Middle Eastern literature should not be confused with ethnography and yet, many Western readers read it as such and have done so for decades. Here more than in any other of his novels, Zaghmout does not let us forget that sexual rights and human rights are inextricably linked and the issues pertaining to these rights are of universal concern.

In her book *Bad Girls of the Arab World* (2017), Jordanian literary scholar Rula Quawas is critical of those individuals in Arab societies who are actually the "maintainers and keepers of traditional values which they fail to recognize as arbitrary" (27). Quawas's observation is exactly what motivates Zaghmout to adopt the approach that he has in writing *The Man of Middling Height*. Zaghmout has found a most clever way to demonstrate the arbitrariness of traditional values in society and chooses to classify the population by height instead of gender. Is this idea absurd? In any case, Zaghmout convinces us that it is not any more ridiculous than the importance placed upon gender and gender roles in a system to which society has been clinging for centuries. It cannot be denied that half of the population has been assigned power based solely on the genitalia with which they were born.

Keeping in mind that *The Man of Middling Height* finds itself firmly rooted in the genre of speculative fiction, Zaghmout has imagined a parallel universe created to attack the rigid gendered worlds in which we all live. This is an especially helpful technique when analyzing more conservative societies which one might find in the Arab world, but it also allows anyone from any culture to view society through a more objective lens. Zaghmout is one of a few Arab artists and writers who have chosen such an approach to make a bold statement. In summer 2024, the exhibit *ARABOFUTURS: Science Fiction and*

New Imaginaries[2] opened at the Institut du Monde Arabe (IMA) in Paris, France, and it explores the notion of using genres such as speculative and science fictions in Arab art and literature precisely in the manner in which Zaghmout has done. An invitation into the "dreamed worlds of the new Arab imaginings," the exhibit features artistic and literary means of "decolonizing the future." Zaghmout's use of speculative fiction in *The Man of Middling Height* becomes a tool to "subvert globalized codes and aesthetics," allowing them "to question the ideologies they convey or to imagine off-center futures that break with hegemonic discourses" (2024). The IMA exhibit claims that from science fiction, numerous "hybrid, post-human imaginaries" have emerged and this has become a trend for artists and writers of the Arab world since the dawn of the millennium, "exploring 'programmed' futures germinating in our present." This is certainly evident in *The Man of Middling Height*, but also in Zaghmout's most recent futuristic novel, *Hope on Earth*, in which the protagonist is a nonbinary person, born female, but not committed to either gender, and thus choosing male pronouns for the lack of neutral pronouns in the Arabic language. Zaghmout's novels imagine more inclusive

2. *ARABOFUTURS: Science-fiction et nouveaux imaginaires* is a special exhibit featured at the Institut du Monde Arabe (IMA) in Paris from April 23 to January 12, 2025. The link to the exhibit can be found here: https://www.imarabe.org/fr/expositions/arabofuturs -science-fiction-et-nouveaux-imaginaires.

futures, and these are at the heart of *ARABOFUTURS*. Since the year 2000, artists from the Arab world and its diasporas have been using science fiction to explore the flaws in our immediate future and to dream the worlds of tomorrow. Through anticipation, they draw up a straight-forward assessment of the evolution of our current societies, questioning the present and transgressing it (2024).[3]

What is revolutionary about Zaghmout's novel translated here is that it does not present a binary society. That is, "talls" and "shorts" in the novel are not just simply replacements for men and women. The presentation of his characters is much more complex and nuanced than this, which is what makes this novel so intriguing to read. Zaghmout has provided readers with an absolutely brilliant way of introducing gender fluidity in Middle Eastern literature; the protagonist Tallan, for example, is "neither tall nor short" (40): "He was not like a needle. Nor was he a thimble. Thus, he was not fit to play a role in the construction of our social fabric" (40).

The Man of Middling Height might be Zaghmout's most innovative work to date. For those who have no knowledge of the Arabic language, it is impossible to fully understand just how difficult it was for Zaghmout to essentially modify the gendered contexts in the Arabic

---

3. This quote is featured on the introductory wall panels of the exhibit *ARABOFUTURS* at the IMA in Paris. It mentions "science fiction," keeping in mind that futuristic genres and speculative fiction were once categorized under science fiction. We see the progression of those genres within the actual exhibit.

language and still have the novel make sense. Likewise, it was no simple feat on the part of the translator, Wasan Abdelhaq, and text editor, Fil Inocencio Jr., to capture and fine-tune all the nuances from the original Arabic, since English has its own gendered patterns that are at times not even remotely comparable to Arabic. For those readers familiar with Arab societies, certain details are readily recognizable (the tendency to frown upon public displays of affection, the notion of marriage as essential to maintaining the fabric of society, the widespread unacceptability of assuming a gender that is not yours at birth, illustrated in the novel as the rejection of those who "feel tall" even if they are not, etc.). Yet, Zaghmout achieves his aim to make everyone at least somewhat uncomfortable with the way we classify people in society; we are all made to recognize our faults and the devastating consequences that they have.

There is literally no other literary work quite like this particular novel—neither in the Arab world nor outside of it. Zaghmout's novel not only allows us to meander around certain societal taboos in order to more openly discuss them, but it also shows us that the identities we have assigned to others are nonsensical. In the worst-case scenario, as is illustrated in *The Man of Middling Height,* this absurdity can provoke violence and claim many victims. With this novel, Fadi Zaghmout has once again demonstrated his brilliance and versatility as a writer, experimenting with literary genres and succeeding in conveying the message that has always been a hallmark of his work.

Works Cited

Alsanea, Rajaa. 2005. *Banāt al-Riyāḍ*. Dar al-Saqi.

Alsanea, Rajaa. 2007. *Girls of Riyadh*, trans. by Rajaa Alsanea and Marilyn Booth. Penguin Books.

ARABOFUTURS: science-fiction et nouveaux imaginaires. April 23, 2024–Jan. 12, 2025, Institut du Monde Arabe, Paris.

Chreiteh, Alexandra. 2009. *Dā'iman Coca-Cola*. Arab Scientific Publishers.

Chreiteh, Alexandra. 2010. *ʿAlī wa-ummuhu al-Rūsīyah*. Arab Scientific Publishers.

Chreiteh, Alexandra. 2012. *Always Coca-Cola*, trans. by Michelle Hartman. Interlink.

Chreiteh, Alexandra. 2015. *Ali and His Russian Mother*, trans. by Michelle Hartman. Interlink.

Mandour, Sarah. 2010. *32*. Dar Al-Adab.

Mandour, Sarah. 2016. *32*, trans. by Nicole Fares. Syracuse University Press.

Quawas, Rula. 2017. "Inciting Critique in the Feminist Classroom." *Bad Girls of the Arab World* by Nadia Yaqub and Rula Quawas, eds. University of Texas Press, 21–36.

Yaqub, Nadia, and Rula Quawas, eds. 2017. *Bad Girls of the Arab World*. University of Texas Press.

Zaghmout, Fadi. 2012. *Aroos Amman*. Jabal Amman Publishers.

Zaghmout, Fadi. 2012. *The Bride of Amman,* trans. by Ruth Kemp. Signal 8 Press.

Zaghmout, Fadi. 2015. *Janna Ala Al Ard*. Dar Al Adab.

Zaghmout, Fadi. 2017. *Heaven on Earth*, trans. by Sawad Hussain. Signal 8 Press.

Zaghmout, Fadi. 2017. *Laila wal Hamal*. Kotob Khan Publishing.

Zaghmout, Fadi. 2020. *Ebra Wa Kushtuban*. Al-Ahleyya.

Zaghmout, Fadi. 2020. *Laila*, trans. by Hajer Almosleh. Signal 8 Press.

Zaghmout, Fadi. 2023. *Amal Ala Al Ard*. Dar Al Ahleyya.

Appendix

As you reach the end of this story, the linguistic challenge it presents becomes clearer. It is a twofold challenge: The first was translating the height-based language into Arabic language, the original language the story was written in. The second was translating the story from Arabic to English.

For English readers we had two options to follow:

1. *Keep Arabic linguistics as the base of the height-based language:* This would require the narrator to state that she created the Arabic language as a counter language to the height-based language of her world. In this case, the English translation would keep the Arabic references in order to make sense of how the language was developed. In the end we felt that this would not make sense to those who do not have a strong understanding of Arabic.

2. *Make English linguistics the base of the height-based language:* Focus on the universality of the story since all current human societies have gender as the main dividing attribute. In this case, the narrator would be inventing English as a language to counter the height-based language. This would require tailoring language references in the story to adhere to English structures.

We opted for option 2 because we wanted to address the universality of gender rather than focus on the specifics of languages. This proved to be a challenging exercise since English is both structurally and grammatically different and is less gendered than Arabic.

Arabic Language

While writing the Arabic, the author kept in mind the following gender structures:

1. Words are feminized by adding the letter "circular ta'" (ة) at the end of the words. When it is plural feminine, then the "noon" (ن) is added.
2. The "You" pronoun in Arabic has masculine and feminine forms, both in singular and plural forms: "Ant(a)" for masculine singular and "Ant(i)" for feminine singular; "Ant(om)" for masculine plural and "Ant(onna)" for feminine plural.
3. Plurals in general for words follow three rules: masculine plural (jame' mozakkar salem) by adding "waw + noon" (واو + نون) or "ya + noon" (ياء + نون) to the end of the singular, or feminine plural (jame' mo'annath salem) by replacing the circular ta' at the end of the word with "Alef + ta'" (ألف + تاء), or genderless plural that doesn't follow the two rules (jame' takseer) and changes the structure of the word.

Since Arabic uses suffixes to distinguish between the masculine and the feminine, it was imagined that the height-based language uses similar suffixes to distinguish between shorts and talls. In this case, the author opted to add the suffix "ya' + ra'" (ياء + راء) to refer to shorts, and suffix "ya' + lam" (ياء + لام) to refer to talls. Similarly, the author imagined applying related suffixes to words to address the three issues dealing with gender as outlined earlier.

English Language

In English, the language and word structure had to be reimagined.

1. We came up with shorts and talls to refer to the plural social types of short and tall people. Interesting enough, Arabic allows for the plural description of people as shorts and talls (Kesar and Tewaal) without needing to follow it with the word people. Despite Arabic being deemed as a gendered language, it still allows for height-based identities. In English, we had to come up with shorts and talls as identities to avoid using "short people" and "tall people."

2. While English rarely uses suffixes to give a gender dimension to words except for certain professions, it still has gender engraved in words that define human relations, such as kinship terms and social roles. This had to be reflected in the height-based language. In this case, we opted to use "T" and "S" at the beginning of word in the height-based language to point to shortness and tallness.

3. We noticed that many professions add gender to the words in the form of a suffix such as policeman, fireman, businessman, etc. We opted to replace "man" with "short" in the height-based language.

4. We mapped men into shorts and women into talls. For children, since they are all shorts, we opted to keep both boys and girls as children in this world.

5. We outlined personal and impersonal pronouns and reflected gender into height where necessary.

Following are some samples to show what the narrator did in order to transform her height-based language into English linguistics.

1
Social Types (Adults)

Type	People below 167 cm	People between 168 and 181 cm	People above 182 cm	Genitalia Lower Body	Ambiguous Genitalia	Genitalia Upper Body
Social Type Singular	Short	Medium	Tall	Man	Queer	Woman
Social Type Plural	Shorts	Mediums	Talls	Men	Queers	Women
Biological Kind Singular	Short	Average Height person	Tall	Male	Intersex	Female
Biological Kind Plural	Shorts	Average Height people	Talls	Males	Intersex	Females

2
Social Types (Under Age/Under Height)

Type	People below 167 cm	Genitalia Lower Body	Ambiguous Genitalia	Genitalia Upper Body
Social Type Singular	Child	Boy	Queer	Girl
Social Type Plural	Children	Boys	Queers	Girls
Biological Kind Singular	Child	Male	Intersex	Female
Biological Kind Plural	Children	Males	Intersex	Females

3
Personal and Impersonal Pronouns

Person	Number and Gender/Height	Subject	Object	Possessive	Reflexive
First	Singular	I	Me	Mine	Myself
	Plural	We	Us	Ours	Ourselves
Second	Singular	You	Yours	Yourself	
	Plural			Yourselves	
Third	Masculine Singular	He	Him	His	Himself
	Shortness Singular	She	Shim	Shis	Shimself
	Feminine Singular	She	Her	Hers	Herself
	Tallness Singular	Te	Ter	Ters	Terself
	Neutral Singular	It		Its	Itself
	Plural	They	Them	Theirs	Themselves
Impersonal	N/A	One		N/A	Oneself

4
Kinship Terms

Family Member	Short	Tall	Male	Female
Parent	Shather	Tother	Father	Mother
Child	Shon	Taughter	Son	Daughter
Grandparent	Grandshon	Grandtaughter	Grandfather	Grandmother
Sibling	Shrother	Tister	Brother	Sister
Sibling Children	Shephew	Tiece	Nephew	Niece
Parent Sibling	Shuncle	Taunt	Uncle	Aunt
Grandparent Sibling	Great Shuncle	Great Taunt	Great Uncle	Great Aunt

5
Professions/Positions Examples

Professions/Positions	Short	Tall	Male	Female
Monarchy Heads	Shing	Tueen	King	Queen
Monarchy Children	Shrince	Trincell	Prince	Princess
A Person Who Acts	Shactor	Tactrell	Actor	Actress
A Person Who Serves in a Restaurant	Shaiter	Taitrell	Waiter	Waitress
A Person Responsible for Maintaining Public Order	Shortpolice	Tallpolice	Policeman	Policewoman
A Skilled Manual Worker	Shortcraft	Tallcraft	Craftsman	Craftswoman

Fadi Zaghmout is a Jordanian author and sexual freedoms and body rights advocate. He holds an MA in creative writing and critical thinking from Sussex University in the United Kingdom. He has five published novels: *The Bride of Amman, Heaven on Earth, Laila, The Man of Middling Height,* and *Hope on Earth*. His work has been translated into English, French, and Italian. He was winner of the Study UK Alumni Social Action Award in the UAE in 2024.

Wasan Abdelhaq is an experienced translator with a deep passion for bridging cultures through language. With over fifteen years of expertise in translating Arabic to English across a variety of genres, Wasan has contributed to numerous projects, bringing nuanced stories to life for a global audience. She is deeply committed to preserving the authenticity and essence of the original text.